"I'm spending the night."

Anise's fingers flew to her throat. "That isn't necessary. I don't need a babysitter—"

"I know that," Bishop answered, his voice calm and relaxed. "But you were clearly frightened or you wouldn't have called me in the first place. Why not let me sleep on the couch?" He grinned unexpectedly. "I promise I'll stay there unless you'd prefer a different arrangement."

Something entered her expression and then it was gone. He told himself it was his imagination. Breaking every rule he'd ever heard about maintaining personal distance, he put his hand on her cheek. "Let me stay, Anise."

"It's not part of your job description and I'm a big girl. I can take care of myself."

"But maybe I'd *like* to take care of you. Have you considered that?"

To his surprise, she nodded. And it was his turn to raise an eyebrow.

"But I don't want to want that," she said quietly. "Do you understand what I'm saying?"

"Yes, I do. But I think you're wrong. It's okay to need someone on occasion."

She stared at him for a moment, then reached up and hooked her hand behind his head, pulling him closer. "I think *you're* wrong," she said, "but for one tiny second I'm going to pretend that's not the case."

Then her lips closed over his.

Dear Reader,

In *Safe in His Arms*, Anise Borden has two havens of safety—her friendship with Sarah Levy and her work. Anise was raised by Sarah's parents following the tragic loss of her mother in a house fire. The two girls share a relationship that is special to them both. As an adult, Anise finds peace by dedicating herself to her artistic creations, the shadow boxes she sells through Sarah's art gallery. When she is troubled or confused, she turns to these two outlets, sometimes consciously, sometimes not, for comfort and reassurance.

I believe everyone needs a place where they can go and feel safe, a refuge they can retreat to when the world becomes too difficult. For some, that haven may be a physical location: a quiet maze, the beach in winter, a church caught in the ritual of Sunday morning. For others, it may be a state of mind. They lose themselves in a good book or a movie. Sometimes a daydream will suffice. The luckiest of us have found this shelter in the arms of our loving families.

These sanctuaries aren't just for adults, either. Have you ever seen a toddler curled up and asleep under the dining-room table after a chaotic family feast? They're looking for a quiet place in the midst of confusion. Even animals seek places of security. My cats will sometimes hide under the bed when the doorbell rings. They aren't sure who's coming, but they do know where they'll be safe.

In our ever hectic, ever chaotic life, these sanctuaries, be they imaginary or real, are more and more necessary. They keep us sane and balanced. I hope you enjoy Anise's journey to that realization in *Safe in His Arms*, then go on to find your own special place.

Kay David

SAFE IN HIS ARMS
Kay David

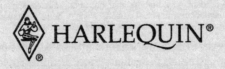

HARLEQUIN®

TORONTO • NEW YORK • LONDON
AMSTERDAM • PARIS • SYDNEY • HAMBURG
STOCKHOLM • ATHENS • TOKYO • MILAN • MADRID
PRAGUE • WARSAW • BUDAPEST • AUCKLAND

ISBN-13: 978-0-373-78162-1
ISBN-10:   0-373-78162-8

SAFE IN HIS ARMS

ABOUT THE AUTHOR

Kay David is the author of over thirty books. She splits her time between the Texas Hill Country and the Gulf coast, where she lives with her husband and her two Bengal cats, Jake and Elwood.

Books by Kay David

HARLEQUIN SUPERROMANCE
798–THE ENDS OF THE EARTH
823–ARE YOU MY MOMMY?
848–THE MAN FROM HIGH MOUNTAIN
888–TWO SISTERS
945–OBSESSION
960–THE NEGOTIATOR*
972–THE COMMANDER*
985–THE LISTENER*
1045–MARRIAGE TO A STRANGER
1074–DISAPPEAR
1131–THE TARGET*
1149–THE SEARCHERS
1200–SILENT WITNESS
1230–THE PARTNER
1303–NOT WITHOUT HER SON**
1321–NOT WITHOUT THE TRUTH**
1338–NOT WITHOUT CAUSE**

SIGNATURE SELECT SAGA
NOT WITHOUT PROOF**

*The Guardians
**The Operatives

Don't miss any of our special offers. Write to us at the following address for information on our newest releases.

Harlequin Reader Service
U.S.: 3010 Walden Ave., P.O. Box 1325, Buffalo, NY 14269
Canadian: P.O. Box 609, Fort Erie, Ont. L2A 5X3

PROLOGUE

Houston, Texas
August 1982

HER EYES WERE OPEN but she couldn't see.

Huddled in her bed, eight-year-old Anise lifted her fingers in front of her face and wiggled them. She actually *could* see them if she narrowed her eyes and wrinkled her nose but something wasn't right.

Because she couldn't breathe any better than she could see. The air in her tiny bedroom was hot and smoky. Sometimes at night her mom cut the AC off to save money but the heat Anise felt now wasn't like that. This was really, really…hot.

The realization was slow in coming but when it came, it hit her hard.

She sat up and blinked, her chest aching,

her arms and legs unwilling to move. Her teacher had talked about this once at school. What to do if you were trapped in a fire. They'd read a book about a little boy who climbed out his bedroom window. He'd run down the street and gotten help but Anise couldn't do that. She was on the second floor.

"Mommy?" Her voice sounded fuzzy. She tried again, this time forcing the word out a little louder. "Mommy?"

Her mother didn't come but the act of speaking freed Anise from the fear that was holding her down. She sprang from the tangle of sheets and leapt across the room, the wooden floor scorching her toes.

"Mommy? Mommy?" She was yelling by the time she got to the door, her feet doing a painful dance. Her fingers found the doorknob and she gripped it hard.

A blistering heat instantly fused her tender palms to the metal. She shrieked then jerked away to stare in horror at her hands; the skin was curling back like waxed paper freshly cut from a roll. She screamed even louder.

But nobody heard.

Panic took over. Her palms throbbing, her lungs burning, Anise darted through the darkness to the corner of her room and wrenched open her closet door using the tips of her fingers. The smoke had yet to reach the confines of the closet and she gulped the air as she dropped to her knees. Crawling to the back, she drew the clothes around her in a futile attempt to hide from the growing heat, her sobs wracking her body. She cradled her hands against her chest.

"Mommy, Mommy, Mommy…"

But it wasn't her mommy who carried her out.

It was Sarah who saved her. Again and again and again.

CHAPTER ONE

Houston, Texas
May 2007

SHE SHOULD HAVE parked closer. By the time Anise reached the gallery, the makeup she'd applied an hour before was sliding off her face. Summers in Houston were brutal but heading for a meeting with a soon-to-be ex-husband didn't help matters.

She had no reason to be nervous, she told herself, pulling open the door to the Levy Gallery. Kenneth had finally agreed that the time had come to part ways and he'd promised to sign the papers when they met for drinks this evening. He wasn't happy about the situation—who ever was happy about divorce?—but he'd assured her there would be no more delays. He accepted the fact that their short marriage was over.

Or so he said.

She stepped into the frigid art gallery and paused under a black vent pouring out icy air. Sarah was nowhere to be seen, but Anise could hear her best friend. She let the cold blast wash over her cheeks and closed her eyes for a second.

"This isn't the right piece for you, Mrs. Worthington, and I'll tell you exactly why." Sarah's voice was full of authority. "Your home is a reflection of your standing in the community. You and Mr. Worthington are stars in the Houston galaxy. You need important art on your walls. Art that demands attention and expects to receive it. You represent the old guard. You can afford the most expensive things. Why not buy them?"

Anise could hear the murmur of another woman's voice but her words were indistinct.

"Yes," Sarah replied, her tone on the verge of condescension. "You're correct there. Borden's pieces *are* developing a following. But you don't need something from an artist who's *developing*. You require art from people who've already arrived. Anise's shadow boxes are almost there, but not quite." Sarah's voice faded as she directed the customer to another part of the gallery.

Anise walked to the corner where Sarah and the woman had obviously been viewing her work. More than once, Sarah had explained her reasons for discouraging people from buying Anise's creations but Anise wasn't sure she agreed with the technique. A sale was a sale and she could always use the money. Sarah was in charge of the business end, though, so Anise handled her concern like she did everything that distracted her, by placing it into a box of its own and filing it in the back of her mind.

She focused instead on the display before her. A single black wall hung in front of her, suspended from chains that stretched into the darkness overhead. It swung gently in the air-conditioning. Six black pedestals made of iron were set before it with six spotlights shining down, one light on each stand.

Sitting on top of each plinth was a box. They ranged in size from six inches square to more than a foot. The bottoms were fashioned from wood but the sides and front were made of glass that had been smeared with petroleum jelly. It was impossible to view the interiors distinctly but inside each box were various items that expressed a theme. Resurrection. Absence. Light. Death. No one knew the titles, but in her mind that's what she called them.

She'd sold her first one six years ago for a few hundred dollars. Sarah never let them go now for under five figures.

Anise heard the front door open and close, its chimes sounding softly. Sarah's quick step came next, her progress audible as she cut through the gallery. Like a miniature whirlwind, Sarah projected energy and power, from her mass of dark, curly hair to the brightly colored suits she favored. There were days when just looking at Sarah made Anise tired.

"I thought that was you who came in." She wrapped Anise in a quick hug then let her go. "Guess you heard me not make a sale for you, huh?"

"As a matter of fact, I did hear what

you told that poor woman." Anise made a wry face. "What do you mean I'm still 'developing?' If I had an ego, it might be a little bruised."

Sarah tossed her head, her hair shimmering under the halogen lights. "We've talked about this before, Anise. That old witch wouldn't know a Van Gogh if it bit her on the butt. I can't let someone like her have one of your pieces."

"I appreciate the sentiment," Anise answered, "but I'm not sure Kenneth would agree."

At the mention of Anise's almost ex-husband's name, Sarah's face darkened but the expression came and went so fast, no one except Anise would have caught it.

"Louisa Worthington is eighty-five, if she's a day. We want the younger crowd buying you. Her patronage would be the kiss of death. If word got out she was acquiring you, anyone with half a brain would run the other way."

She took a breath and continued before Anise could comment.

"You *have* money. You *need* cachet. It's

more important that we build your name. And to build your name, we have to make your boxes exclusive. I'd be happy to explain that concept to Kenneth. Even an asshole like him should be able to understand it."

Anise ignored the name-calling. Sarah had never made her disapproval of Kenneth a secret. "I'm on my way to meet him. Why don't you come with me and the two of you can argue about it?" Anise teased instead. "I'd rather listen to you guys fight than talk about the divorce."

"But he already agreed to everything, didn't he?" Sarah's eyes widened, an instant's gleam of alarm coming into them. "I thought you said he'd told you—"

Anise held up her hand. "He agreed, but you know how Kenneth can be. I wouldn't be surprised if he changed his mind at the last minute and said no again."

"He better not if he knows what's good for him." Stepping closer to one of the shadow boxes, Sarah adjusted it as she rejected Anise's words. "This whole mess was Kenneth's fault from the very beginning." She tightened her lips, two angry lines forming around her mouth. "He's an idiot and he has never appreciated you or your work. You're amazing and he can't see that. If there's a failure here, it's his, not yours."

Anise reached out and squeezed Sarah's hand. "I don't deserve a friend as good as you."

"You're right," Sarah retorted. "You *don't* deserve me but unfortunately for you, I'm all you've got."

Anise and Sarah had been more than best friends since elementary school when Anise's single mother had died in a house fire. Abraham and Rachel, Sarah's parents and the Bordens' next-door neighbors at the time, took Anise into their home and their family, and she'd been there ever since. After Abe had died and Rachel retired, Sarah had taken over the gallery even though she'd only been twenty-five.

Despite their closeness, Anise and Sarah were very different from one another, their opposing sexual orientation the least of it. Anise was the artist but she wasn't a flamboyant diva. She had barely dated before marrying Kenneth and her favorite evening was a quiet one by the fire with a good book. Sarah was never at home and she went through relationships like candy, the women in her world forming an ever-changing parade. She couldn't seem to settle down with one person. Neither could Anise, but their reasons were as different as their lovers.

"Which just means you *should* go with me tonight," Anise replied. "What kind of friend would make me do this alone?"

Sarah shook her head. "Can't oblige, sorry. Robin's coming over—" She glanced down at her watch. "In fact, she should be here by now. We're going out ourselves."

"You could bring her with us. The more the merrier?"

Sarah shook her head. "I don't think so. Robin sees enough of Kenneth at the office. Another hour might just put her over the edge."

Anise nodded. Sarah's on-again, off-again lover, Robin Estes, worked as Kenneth's assistant. In fact, Robin was the one who'd introduced Anise and her husband two years before when she'd brought the handsome tax attorney to one of Anise's shows. They'd hit it off and before she'd known what she was doing, Anise had accepted his proposal, their whirlwind romance and impulsive elopement the only hasty decision she'd ever made in her life.

Anise sighed dramatically. "All right. I guess I'm going to have to tackle this one on my own."

"You'll do fine." As they walked toward the front door, Sarah spoke with even more conviction than she'd used when she'd been talking to her customer earlier. "Getting rid of Kenneth is the absolute right thing to do. You won't regret it for a minute." She swung the door open and the humidity rolled over both of them.

"Maybe." Anise glanced back at her friend. "But I don't intend to go through this kind of turmoil again. It's not worth it."

"Ending a relationship is always tough."

Anise shook her head. "I'm not talking about splitting up. That's the easy part," she said. "Falling in love is what I mean. I don't care who comes along next, I'm sticking with my work. It's never let me down."

ANISE CONTINUED up the street to the restaurant where she was supposed to meet Kenneth. Over the past few years, downtown Houston had made its predictable swing back into popularity, exploding with swanky new spots and upscale restaurants. Anise tended to avoid it. She liked the old places where they knew which table she preferred and what she wanted to eat when she walked in the door. Kenneth had picked the spot tonight, though, and she hadn't cared enough to argue. All she wanted was to put the meeting behind her.

She didn't rush as she walked down the sidewalk. He would be late, because he was always late. She'd use the extra time to gather her thoughts and organize her feelings. She hadn't been lying when she'd told Sarah she felt like a failure. Anise *wasn't* happy with the way her brief marriage had ended but she *was* looking forward to having Kenneth out of her life.

He'd never understood her friendship with Sarah or the time Anise devoted to her art, seeming to be jealous of each, although he'd had no basis in fact for either. They'd argued about it more and more until his constant demands had turned unbearable. At that point, she'd realized that Kenneth's world consisted of Kenneth and no one else. The sun, the moon and the stars all revolved around him. Anything outside of that simply didn't exist. He was never going to change. And neither was she. Her boxes were her life. After a year of marriage, she told him she'd wanted out. He'd fought her for six months and she wasn't sure why but he'd finally come around.

The small restaurant was packed. Had she been on her own, she would have turned around and left but she didn't have that luxury tonight. She gave a groan and fought her way to the hostess stand. To her surprise, Kenneth had made a dinner reservation and the young girl seated her immediately. Even more surprisingly, before Anise could order a drink, Kenneth appeared in the doorway. He waved to her, then started across the crowded room.

Most of the women, and some of the men, watched as he came toward her. At six-one, with dark hair, blue eyes and a self-confident air, Kenneth was a handsome man and he knew it. He would be a very eligible bachelor again.

Arriving at their table, he kissed her, smoothed his jacket then slid into the booth beside her. "I'm on time," he announced. "Aren't you proud of me?"

Anise looked at him and shook her head. He actually thought she should be impressed because he had managed the simple courtesy.

The waitress materialized beside their table. She zeroed in on Kenneth and Anise became invisible. Kenneth proceeded to flirt with the woman then ask her which drinks the bartender specialized in. Anise sat quietly and let him have his fun. This was the last time she'd have to put up with it so why not? After a few more minutes of discussion, the waitress wrote something on her pad then waded through the throng to the bar.

Kenneth turned to Anise. "I'm sure you'll like the Cosmos. That's what she recommended and I've heard they really are the best—"

"I could care less what we drink, Kenneth. I'm here for one thing and that's to get these papers signed." Anise went for her purse but Kenneth stopped her, his hand on her arm.

"Can't that wait a bit?"

She raised her eyes to his and started to argue but behind the polished facade Kenneth wore like a second skin, a glimmer of something unfamiliar caught her attention. It looked like anxiety but she decided she was wrong. Kenneth didn't worry about anything, including his practice. His ability to navigate the federal tax law labyrinth was amazing but he had never pushed himself to build his clientele. He puttered along, making a mediocre amount but living large.

"I'll sign them," he promised, "But first I need a few minutes to catch my breath. It was a hell of a day." He put his cell phone on the table between them. "Hope you don't mind, but I'm expecting a call I need to catch…"

Before Anise could reply, the waitress reappeared. She held a tray with two glistening drinks on it, their color matching her nail polish so perfectly Anise wondered if she'd planned it. With a flourish she put the drinks down then walked away, sending Kenneth a smile over her shoulder he didn't catch.

It *had* to have been a bad day for Kenneth to miss that....

Anise's mind skipped over the probable causes before it landed on the most obvious reason. "Is it Brittany?" she asked. "Is she okay?"

Kenneth's previous marriage had produced a daughter. Wild and unpredictable, Brittany had been a huge source of problems for Kenneth over the past sixteen years. Her latest round with drugs and alcohol would have been a cliché had the situation not been so serious.

"Brittany hasn't been okay since she was two," Kenneth said wearily.

His truthful reply surprised her. Despite Anise's numerous attempts to make him see things differently, Kenneth generally tried to downplay his daughter's "growing pains," as he put them.

"What's wrong?"

"What's always wrong with Brittany? It's her mother, of course." He picked up his drink and half emptied it, the thought of his first wife apparently leaving him with the urge to get drunk.

Anise could appreciate the sentiment.

Donna Capanna was an angry woman and she didn't bother to hide it. She and Kenneth had already been divorced when she found out he and Anise were marrying, but she'd been upset and resentful. Her irrational reaction had been bad enough, but she'd infected her daughter with her poisonous feelings, turning the girl against Kenneth as well. Anise had been appalled. What kind of woman used a child—her *own* daughter at that—as a weapon?

"She's demanding I put another ten thousand into Brittany's college fund." Kenneth stared into his drink and shook his head. "We'll be lucky if Britt gets out of high school. I don't know where Donna's coming from."

"Have you talked to her about it?"

"Talk to Donna? Are you kidding? That paint you use must be getting to your brain." He caught the waitress's eye and twirled his finger for another round. "She's too busy playing with her latest conquest to talk about her daughter. You should know that by now."

Anise squirmed. Discussing Kenneth's ex, no matter how irresponsible she was, had never made Anise comfortable and now, she was about to earn that label herself. She would be the "ex." She flashed ahead five years and imagined Kenneth sitting in another booth with another woman talking about Anise. "She was crazy," he would pronounce. She imagined him twirling that same finger in a circular motion only this time beside his ear. "An artist. A real nutcase…"

"…damn business doing just about as bad, too. Robin's driving me nuts. I don't know what the hell's happening with my life."

Anise blinked and came back to the moment. "Why is Robin upset? What's wrong at work?"

His lips tightened with anger. "I just told you," he said, his attitude nudging its way past edginess and into impatience. "You weren't even listening, were you? Some things never change."

"Tell me again," she said.

Staring at her, he downed the rest of his drink then picked up the second one the waitress had delivered, his irritation deflating as quickly as it had come.

"It's nothing," he said with a wave of his hand. "It doesn't matter."

Anise started to press him, then stopped.

The problem he had was most likely the same one that he usually had.

Kenneth was always broke.

The whole time they'd lived together, Anise had supported them. The money he made seemed to evaporate. Sarah had continually tried to get Anise to make Kenneth cut back, but she had never been successful.

He grinned, his mood shifting again as he put his arm on the back of the booth, his eyes falling on her face. "You didn't come here to listen to me complain, did you? You came here to get rid of my sorry ass...."

Anise returned his smile before she could help herself. He could be so charming when he wanted to be. "I wouldn't put it that way…."

"But…"

"But I do need your signature on some things, Kenneth. It's time. We've gone over the details enough and my attorney is ready to move on. He wants to file next week. You have to sign these papers before we can do that."

He leaned across the table and put his hands on hers. "I think you're making a mistake," he said. "I think *we're* making a mistake. I still love you, baby. And you love me. We could make this work if we tried a little harder."

"That's not going to happen, Kenneth, and you know it. Don't do this."

He stared at her a moment longer, then he leaned back and pressed his spine against the soft leather booth, his gaze distant, his mood swinging this time to thoughtfulness. Kenneth usually stayed on a pretty even keel but he was making her nervous tonight. The idea crossed her mind that he might even be taking something. It wouldn't be the first time. For another two seconds, he simply sat there, then he seemed to wake up. Thrusting his hand inside his coat pocket, he pulled out the black Mont Blanc she'd given him for their first anniversary. The irony apparently escaped him.

"Where do I sign?"

She removed the sheaf of blue-covered documents from her purse and pointed to the spots her attorney's secretary had flagged. Kenneth scratched his signature on each line without comment then capped the pen. His gaze met hers. "So that's it?"

She nodded.

He waited a beat and for some reason she thought he might kiss her but he reached for his wallet instead. Throwing some bills on the table, he slid out of the booth then held his hand to hers. Surprised by his readiness to leave but too grateful to question it, she stood as well.

"Let me walk you to your car," he said.

"That's not necessary…."

"I know it's not," he answered, "but I want to."

She hesitated because of his erratic behavior then chastised herself. He was upset and had had a bad day but he was trying to be nice. What was her problem? "Sure," she said. "That'd be fine…."

"Great. I'll just be a minute." He headed for the rear of the restaurant where the restrooms were located, the crowd swallowing him. Before Anise could decide to wait outside or in, a cell phone started to ring. The sound drew her eyes to the table they'd just vacated. Kenneth's black Motorola was still on the marble top. He'd forgotten it.

She debated whether or not to answer, then remembered what he'd said about a phone call. It might be Brittany. She'd hate for the girl to think he was ignoring her. Misunderstandings like that fed right into Donna's lies. Anise picked up the phone and hit the receive button. An angry female voice buzzed in her ear.

"You aren't going to get away with this, Kenneth. I know what you're trying to do and it's not going to happen. I don't give a damn what else is going on, I've had enough. I'm ready for this to stop and I'm not kidding this time!"

The venom behind the speaker's voice shocked Anise into silence. She'd never heard anyone speak with such virulent rage.

The caller continued, the malice only growing more intense. "I'll see you dead first, Kenneth. I swear to God, I'll see you dead. And that's not a threat...it's a promise."

CHAPTER TWO

THE LINE WENT SILENT after that.

Standing in the center of the now-packed bar, Anise closed the phone to stare at the blinking display. A single word filled the caller ID screen. *Private.*

The next instant the hostess went by, a cadre of laughing women following her to the table Anise and Kenneth had just abandoned. Moving as quickly as she could, Anise waded through the crowd and stepped outside. The muggy air she'd cursed thirty minutes before suddenly felt good. She was chilled, she realized, even a little shaky.

Who on earth would want to say such vicious things to Kenneth? What had he gotten himself into? Was his business situation that bad? She wished she'd listened closer even though it wasn't really her problem anymore. Maybe his money troubles were more serious than she'd thought. The idea took her straight to Donna. Had it been her? Anise bit her bottom lip and tried to recall the voice but she'd been so surprised by the words she hadn't concentrated on the speaker. She couldn't discount Brittany, either. More than once, she'd heard the girl refer to her father by his given name. With the instinctive cruelty of a teenager she'd known calling him Kenneth would hurt him.

But a death threat was pretty serious. Even for Brittany.

Anise heard her name and turned in time to see Kenneth pushing his way out the door. "My God, it's getting packed in there," he said as he reached her side. "Where did all these people come from?"

She shook her head; then a stretch SUV pulled to the curb right in front of them and disgorged a group of kids who headed en masse to the restaurant behind them. The boys were wearing tuxes and the girls had on matching satin and silk, their hair upswept, their makeup sparkling. A *quinceañera,* Anise thought with distraction. The teens forced Kenneth and Anise apart for a moment before he found her again and took her elbow, laughing as he did so. "What a crowd…"

"Listen, Kenneth, while you were in the restroom, your phone rang. You said you were expecting a call and I thought it might be Brittany so I answered it, but maybe I shouldn't have…." She handed him his phone then hesitated. She didn't even know how to explain.

"Who was it?"

"I don't know." She licked her lips and relayed the conversation. "Whoever it was was very upset."

To her surprise, he blew it off. "I've got an unhappy client. She hasn't paid her taxes in four years and she refuses to understand why I can't get the IRS off her back," he explained. "It's not important. She calls me all the time and threatens to do stuff."

"She sounded serious this time."

"She is," he grinned.

"Aren't you worried?"

"She'll get over it." He paused and gave her a rueful smile. "It's not like she's getting a divorce or something."

"Oh, Kenneth…" Anise rolled her eyes at his drama. "You're going to be fine. In fact, you'll be better off without me. Let's just say goodbye—"

He put a finger against her lips, his eyes turning dark, the noise of the people around them fading as they stared at each other. "Don't say it, Anise. Please… I don't think I can handle it if you say goodbye."

His plea stunned her. He sounded genuine.

"Just let me kiss you, okay? Let's leave it at that. I won't ask you for anything else, I promise."

Without waiting for her answer, he pulled her to him, his embrace as warm as it'd ever been, the scent of his aftershave bringing with it memories she didn't want. Their lips met just as a crack rang out.

A second later, Kenneth slumped against her. Puzzled by his actions, Anise struggled to stay upright but he weighed too much and they both went down, Anise crying out as she hit the sidewalk, her ankle twisting beneath her at an awkward angle.

She didn't understand what had happened until she saw the blood.

DANIEL BISHOP STEPPED through the front door of his two-bedroom apartment just as the phone on his belt began to ring. One of the rookies had slipped a bright red plastic cover on it the day before and Bishop couldn't peel the damned thing off. It looked like a phone a working girl would carry, but for the time being he was stuck. He yanked the phone off his belt, stared at the display, then cursed as he read the number. But he answered it.

"Bishop."

"We got a body downtown, corner of Smith and Rusk streets." Rudy Castillo sounded bored. "White male, DOA, name of Kenneth Capanna. He was an attorney so don't screw anything up. The uniforms are waiting. Wits on site."

The cop shop was so close his captain could have jumped out his window and landed in the intersection he'd just named but Bishop didn't point that out. Investigators who did things like that ended up getting even more calls. "I'm on my way." He pivoted then found his progress blocked by Blanco, his eighty-five-pound yellow Labrador.

"I'm sorry, buddy." Bishop bent over and stroked the animal's head. "I got a dead lawyer off Smith. I'll call Brenda for you, okay?"

The dog seemed to sigh, which Bishop took as an exasperated okay. Opening his front door, Bishop called the girl down the street who walked the dog when Bishop couldn't. She agreed to take him out as Bishop climbed back inside his Crown Vic. The seat was still hot as he started the engine. It was May in Houston. Everything was hot. The city had already had more murders than it had had by the middle of last year and there didn't appear to be an end in sight. Every HPD cop Bishop knew had more cases than he could handle.

He put the car in gear and headed out. Twenty minutes later he reached downtown, lights from half a dozen cop cars bouncing off the offices and restaurants and bars that lined the busy area. Parking as close as he could, Bishop flashed his gold badge at the uniforms guarding the perimeter. They lifted the tape and let him in. The jagged gasps of a crying woman cut through the warm night air. She sounded out of control and he winced.

"Who's bawling?"

Jackie Hunter lifted her head as Bishop spoke, one camera in her hand, two more strung around her neck. She snapped another picture of the body stretched out on the sidewalk then answered. "One of the waitresses is grief-stricken. Apparently they got real close when she took his drink order." The crime scene tech used one of her cameras to point south of where they stood "*That's* the widow."

A fancy upholstered chair had been hauled out of the restaurant and set in front of the valet's stand. Between the milling cops and frightened witnesses, the woman who occupied it looked as incongruent as the chair itself. Ivory skin, auburn hair, an ethereal air... Except for the splash of red that stained her white jacket. She should have been in a church, Bishop thought unexpectedly, frozen over the altar, her hands crossed over her chest. He'd never seen anyone sit so still. Especially at a murder scene.

When their husband was dead on the ground ten feet away.

He filed away the image for future examination. "Who was the responding?"

Hunter flapped a hand toward a group of uniformed officers huddled beside the curb. One of them lifted his head at the movement and peeled away from the others to come toward them. He was a rookie named Carter and he did good work. Shaking Bishop's hand, the cop briefed him quickly.

"Witnesses?" Bishop asked when he finished.

"Too many to count," Carter said. "But none of them saw a thing."

"Drive-by?"

"No one noticed a car. Lot of folks milling around, though. Shooter could have disappeared in the crowd and no one would have caught it."

Bishop glanced at the high-rises around them. "You checked out those offices?"

"Doing it right now."

They went over a few more details then Bishop nodded toward the redheaded woman. "I understand that's the widow."

Flipping through the small notebook he'd been consulting, the younger cop read from his notes. "Anise Borden. Self-employed. 6789 Seventeenth Avenue."

"I thought you said they were married."

He looked up from his notes. "They are...or were, I guess I should say. But she uses her name. She's some kinda artist."

"What else?"

"That's it." Carter dropped his voice. "I took a statement from her but maybe you can make more headway. It was 'yes' and 'no' and not much else. She couldn't have plugged the guy herself since she was standing right beside him but she's an icicle."

"Is she in shock?"

"The medics checked her out and said she's fine."

Bishop stared at the widow. "Then I guess I better see what I can do."

"Good luck. I think you're gonna need a blowtorch to thaw that one out."

Bishop made his way toward the woman, stopping first to check with the medical people then talking with some of the other crime scene investigators. He wanted to give her plenty of time. It took some folks longer than others for reality to soak in.

Ten minutes later, when he stood directly before Anise Borden, she lifted her eyes. He would have bet green, but they were blue. A pale, almost colorless blue.

"I'm Daniel Bishop," he said. "Investigator, HPD. People call me Bishop."

She held out her hand and he shook it. In contrast to the rest of her polished perfection, her palm was rough, the skin etched with lines. He wondered about it then spoke. "I'm sorry about what happened here tonight. It's bad enough to lose someone but to have to go through this, too."

"Thank you," she said. Her voice was low and soft, as controlled as her expression. "Can you catch whoever did this?"

"We intend to," he said. "But we'll need your help."

"Of course. I'll do whatever I can."

He studied her as she spoke, the details he'd missed from down the street registering now. Beneath the white jacket, she wore jeans and a black T-shirt. She didn't have on a wedding band, but the rest of her jewelry, a gold chain and hoop earrings, was simple and elegant. He'd dated a woman once who worked at Tiffany's and she'd told him nice jewelry was like a designer swimsuit—the less there was to it, the more it cost. An equally expensive-looking leather handbag sat at Anise Borden's feet. It was covered in blood.

He asked her to tell him what had happened and she did, her manner composed. He interrupted once to ask her to point out where she'd been standing and when she finished, he spoke bluntly.

"I'll need to question you more later but the first thing I want to ask is the most obvious. Do you have any idea who might want him dead?"

She blinked then looked him straight in the eye. "I know exactly who wanted him dead. Unfortunately I don't have a clue what her name is."

THE TALL COP DIDN'T REACT to her words. He simply nodded. "Tell me more."

Anise handed him Kenneth's cell phone. "He got a call right as we were leaving the bar. I answered it because he was in the restroom. It was a woman and she said—no, she promised—she would see him dead."

"That must have been upsetting."

"I was surprised, to say the least. When he came out, I gave him the phone and asked him about it, but he said it wasn't important. He said he had a client who was in trouble with the IRS and she'd been threatening him for quite some time."

"What was her name?"

"He didn't tell me. We walked to the curb and then…" She stopped and gathered herself. "Then he was shot."

"What did Mr. Capanna do?"

"He's an attorney. A tax attorney. He helped people manage their income so their taxes would be as low as possible. He assisted with audits and things like that—"

She broke off when she looked at her hands. They were still red with Kenneth's blood, the lines and scars filled with it. If she didn't know better she would have thought she'd been using Gamblin's alizarin crimson with maybe a bit of cadmium red medium thrown in to bring out the blue. The color under her nails would have matched the paint perfectly. Her chest went tight in midbreath, a band of disbelief cutting off air as the cop spoke again.

"Had he lost any big cases lately? Someone who might be mad at him?"

She shrugged in an expression of help-lessness. "I don't know. He said he was having problems at the office but I wasn't listening...."

"What's the name of his firm?"

"He has an office off Richmond and Sage. The name of his company is Capanna and—"

Before she could finish, the sound of Sarah's strident voice cut through the crowd of milling cops and curious by-standers. Anise jumped to her feet, her eyes searching for her friend. A second later she spotted her and began to wave. "Sarah! Over here!"

Sarah started forward but a uniformed woman reached out and stopped her. The argument escalated until Anise turned to the man beside her and put her hand on his arm. "Please tell them it's okay. She's my friend."

He looked over Anise's head and called out someone's name. The cop who'd been restraining Sarah turned, saw Bishop, then lifted the tape. A moment later, Sarah was there, her strong arms wrapping Anise in a hug that almost made her break down. She managed to pull herself together before she did and introduced Sarah to the investigator.

Sarah ignored Bishop. "My God, Anise, what happened? Robin and I were leaving the gallery and the lights caught our attention so we came down to see what was going on. Then I—I saw Kenneth. I don't understand…."

"I don't, either," Anise answered. "We walked outside the restaurant and someone shot him. Just like that. Out of the blue. I…I don't know why or who or—"

The policeman interrupted Anise's stuttering explanation. "I'm sorry, I know this is difficult, but I have to ask you some more questions. Perhaps your friend could wait?"

Sarah turned to the cop with the fury of a mother bear. "You're going to have to ask those questions later, Mr. Bishop. This woman is in shock and I need to get her to a hospital. In fact, I can't believe you're holding her here like this! Can't you see she's shaking?"

Anise tried to intervene but she realized Sarah was right. She had begun to tremble—violently. She clenched her teeth in an effort to make the quivering stop but it didn't work. Lifting her gaze to Bishop's, she spoke. "I…I think Sarah might have a point. Could this wait?"

Anise could see he wanted to refuse, but when their eyes met, he couldn't. A wave of gratitude hit her as he gave in.

"Of course," he said. "We have your address. I'll be by as soon as I finish up here."

THEY ARGUED BRIEFLY over whether or not Anise should go to the hospital. Disagreeing with Sarah was generally a pointless activity but this time, Anise won. She didn't bother to question why; she just closed her eyes and let Sarah drive her home. By the time they arrived, her trembling had subsided but on the inside a sick feeling had started to take hold.

"You go take a hot shower," Sarah instructed once they were inside. "I'll make some tea." She started down the narrow hallway to the kitchen then stopped. "Why don't you give me your clothes? I'll take care of them."

Anise looked down at her bloody jacket. "I can't," she said woodenly. "The police…they want them. Could you get me a paper bag?"

Sarah nodded, then hurried down the hall. When she came back, a brown grocery sack in her hands, Anise was standing in the same spot. Sarah led her to the bathroom. Pulling the shower curtain, she twisted the faucets on full force. "Can you get undressed by yourself?"

"I think so."

"I'll be in the kitchen. Call me if you need me."

"I will."

The door closed behind her and Anise sat down on the toilet, the tiny room filling with steam as her fingers went to her T-shirt and then her jacket. The fabric was stiff but she managed to get the buttons undone. Slipping out of her jeans, she folded everything carefully and put it all in the paper bag. She creased the top of the bag and set it aside.

Nausea swamped her a moment later. She barely had time to get the lid up before the hot gush came. When it was over, she stepped into the shower.

The tears that came next were as unexpected as the vomiting. And just as violent. For a heartbeat, she couldn't catch her breath and that brought with it a claustrophobic panic. Then she gasped loudly and air filled her lungs once again. The last time Anise had cried had been the day of the fire. Crying hadn't helped her then, she'd realized, so why bother? She hadn't shed a single tear over anything since and she tried to keep her emotions in just as tight a check.

Her efforts to stay in control failed her tonight, though, and she didn't know why. Grief wasn't the reaction sweeping over her; she and Kenneth hadn't been close for months. It was simple horror. She couldn't forget the image of him in her arms. The sounds he'd made, the blood everywhere, his body going limp...

She held her face under the showerhead and let the water pelt her. For five minutes she didn't move, then finally she reached for the soap and began to scrub. When she cut off the water and pulled the curtain back, Sarah had opened the door.

She stood on the threshold, a mug in one hand, alarm on her face. She'd obviously heard Anise crying. "Do you want your tea or something else?"

Shaken by the storm still swirling inside her, Anise didn't move. She *couldn't* move. Sarah pulled a towel from the bar beside the shower and handed it to her. "Dry off," she fussed. "You're gonna get chilled."

Anise took the towel from Sarah's hands and dropped her face into its warmth. For a second she hid her face in it, her hair dripping, then she wrapped it around her body and accepted the mug of tea.

Sarah leaned against the door frame, a frown on her forehead. "Are you okay?"

"As okay as I'm going to be, at least for a while." Her voice trailed off and she had to force herself to speak again. "I…I don't even know how I feel, to be honest. It's not like we were still in love or anything but I can't stop shaking. And I keep thinking about what he looked like." She shuddered. "I've never had anyone die in my arms before…."

"I can't believe it even happened." Sarah shook her head. "Who on earth would do such a thing? Do they think it was random or…"

"I don't think they think anything right now," Anise answered. She took a sip of the hot tea, some of her equilibrium returning as she told Sarah about the phone call Kenneth had received. The doorbell rang in the middle of her explanation.

"That's Madelyn. I called her as soon as I could." Sarah straightened then went to open the door for Anise's neighbor.

Madelyn Sutcliff had been friends with Anise and Sarah since they'd met ten years previous. Sarah had taken on one of Madelyn's sculptures to sell and over time, the three had grown close. Madelyn served as the mother figure, the wise older woman, the one who had all the answers. Having a master's degree in counseling helped as well. When she entered Anise's living room a few minutes later, though, she had nothing but questions, her expression pained, her apprehension obvious.

"Oh, Anise…sweetheart! I don't know what to say!" She crossed the room and enveloped Anise in her arms, her touch as comforting as the heavy bathrobe Anise had put on. "I'm so sorry!"

Anise patted Madelyn on the arm. "I'm sorry, too," she said. "It's so awful…."

"Tell me what happened."

The three women took their usual places in Anise's living room but the conversation was so far removed from anything they'd ever discussed before the situation felt surreal. For what was beginning to feel like the hundredth time, Anise explained how

Kenneth had died. Thirty minutes after Madelyn arrived, the doorbell rang again. They looked at each other then Anise spoke. "That's got to be the cop."

"He's just going to have to wait," Sarah announced, jumping up from the couch. "You're exhausted! You can't talk to him now. I'll tell him he has to come back later—"

"No." Anise rose to her feet as well, her answer stopping Sarah's progress toward the door. "I want to get it over with. I'll talk to him."

"I don't think that's a good idea—"

"I know what you think, Sarah. Everyone always knows what you think. But this time, you're wrong. I…I need to talk to him, okay?"

Anyone else would have taken offense at Anise's words; Sarah ignored them. She threw open the front door and glared at the detective on the front porch.

"Anise can't talk to you right now," she said. "She's too upset. You're going to have to come back tomorrow."

Before the man could answer, Anise

came up behind Sarah and put a restraining hand on her shoulder. "That won't be necessary. I can talk to you now." Her eyes met Daniel Bishop's, and underneath her touch, she felt Sarah stiffen.

"That's good." He ignored Sarah as effectively as Anise did, his own gaze steady and direct. "Because tomorrow might be too late. I need some answers tonight if I'm going to catch who did this."

Sarah huffed her indignation. "You can't be serious, Anise! You need to res—"

The investigator's attitude was mellow but beneath it was a subtle strength impossible to dismiss. "I'm going to have to ask you to leave, Ms. Levy. I'm sure you understand why."

"I don't understand at all." Sarah crossed her arms and stood her ground.

Anise felt Madelyn at her elbow. She introduced the older woman to Bishop, then watched as she took Sarah's arm.

"We have to let the man do his work, Sarah. You come to my house. Anise can call us when they finish and we'll come back." She flashed Anise a look of sympathy. "We'll spend the night with you, sweetheart."

"That won't be necessary." Anise leaned over and kissed Sarah on the cheek, then did the same with Madelyn. "I'll be fine. You two go on."

Madelyn nodded but Sarah began to shake her head.

"Leave," Anise said firmly. "I'll call you after we finish."

"You promise?" Sarah asked. "Cross your heart and hope to die? Stick a needle in your eye?"

Anise smiled at the childhood whimsy. How many times had she and Sarah made those pledges to each other? Too many to count, she was sure. She made an X over her chest. "I promise."

Bishop stepped aside and held the door open. Sending him one last glare, Sarah walked past the cop and Madelyn followed.

CHAPTER THREE

"YOUR FRIENDS ARE very protective," Bishop said as soon as the door closed behind the women. "How long have you known each other?"

"Forever." Anise led him into her living room. "Would you like a cup of tea? We were having one when you came."

A drink would have been better but he kept that to himself. "Tea would be nice," he said. "Thank you."

He followed her to the kitchen, taking in the small house as they went down a short hallway. He'd been surprised when he'd learned she lived in the Heights. The modest one-story bungalow was typical for the older neighborhood but he'd mentally put her in a classier, more expensive part of town. A lot of artist types were fond of the area, though, so it made sense.

The hall opened into a galley kitchen, a glass-topped table at one end in front of a wall of windows that revealed a well-tended backyard. She had lights at the base of all the trees. They threw spooky shadows everywhere.

"How long is forever?"

She looked at him over her shoulder. "A very long time. Sarah's parents raised me after my mother died and I met Madelyn through the gallery when I was in my twenties. Sarah owns Levy's Art Gallery downtown and she represents both of us."

"Officer Carter told me you're an artist."

"That's right."

He expected her to elaborate but she didn't so he said nothing more. There would be time for that later. The answers he didn't get usually told him more than the ones he got, regardless.

"You have a nice place here." Turning to the window, he watched her reflection in the glass. She moved with grace as she filled the kettle and gathered the tea supplies. "It's very comfortable. The Heights is getting popular. Prices are rising."

"I bought it ten years ago."

"Was that before you got married?"

As if suddenly remembering why he was there, she stopped and stared at him. "Yes. Kenneth moved in with me. He was in a condo at the time and he sold it." She paused. "His ex got the big house."

Bishop gave her a one-sided smile. "From what I understand that happens a lot. At least that's what *my* ex told me when it came time to divide up the spoils."

Anise Borden returned Bishop's smile but the expression faded quickly. "I need to call her," she said. "Kenneth's ex-wife, I mean. You haven't talked to her, have you?"

"Didn't even know he had one. I'll need her contact information, though, along with a list of anyone else you might think of who could add something to the investigation. If you'd like to phone her first, that's fine."

"Her name is Donna Capanna." She gave him her address and number. "They have a daughter named Brittany. She's sixteen.

I'm not their favorite person but it would probably be better to hear the news from me rather than the television."

"This could be obvious but humor me... why aren't you their favorite person?"

"Donna thinks I stole Kenneth from her."

"Did you?"

"They'd been divorced for two years when Kenneth and I started dating."

"I guess she wasn't ready to turn loose, eh? Especially since she kept his name?"

"You could say that."

"Would *you* say that?"

Her eyes were emotionless as she considered the question. "Donna's a very bitter, unhappy woman. It was easier for her to blame me than to examine their relationship."

"Was she unhappy enough to kill him?"

The candor of his question took her by surprise, which is exactly why he asked it. Her hand snaked up to the lapels of her robe. She hesitated then answered. "I don't think so...but who can say for sure? I have to admit I wondered if that was her on the phone."

"Did the voice sound like hers?"

"I can't say for sure."

"Is she capable of being violent?"

"Maybe. When it comes to money." The teakettle behind her began to whistle and she jumped. Filling two mugs with hot water, she added tea bags, then brought the cups to the table. Bishop pulled out the chair closest to her and sat down himself.

"Did Mr. Capanna and his ex-wife argue over their finances?"

"Constantly. She wanted more of it and he didn't have it."

Bishop cocked his head. "I thought you said he was an attorney?"

"He is…or was." She bit her bottom lip then released it. "But money wasn't something Kenneth handled well. He never had enough of it."

"Why is that?"

"For the same reason most people can't, I suppose. He liked to spend it more than he liked to make it."

"And the former Mrs. Capanna shared this problem?"

"No. Her family has plenty of money

and her parents have always been very generous with her. She liked to use Kenneth's financial situation against him, though. It was a big stick and she could hammer him with it. He told me tonight that she'd just asked him for more to put into Brittany's college fund. He wasn't happy about that."

"He didn't want his daughter to go to college?"

"He didn't think she could make it." She explained the girl's troubled background then said, "Brittany's had a bad go of it but I don't see her shooting her father. Underneath it all, she loves him."

"What about you?" he asked. "Did you love him, too?"

Her expression didn't change. "We were separated. The divorce papers are in my purse. That's the only reason we were together tonight—we met at the bar so Kenneth could sign everything."

He processed the information slowly, her reaction at the crime scene, or lack thereof, making more sense than it had before. "Why didn't you tell me this earlier?"

"I didn't think it mattered."

"I guess I don't understand, then."

"What's not to understand?"

He pulled a spiral notebook from his jacket and thumbed through the pages as if he was looking for something. In reality he was giving himself some time to think. A pending divorce had been the last thing he'd expected but he couldn't say why. Maybe Anise Borden's elegance had gotten to him. The longer he sat in front of her, the more impressive it had become. He couldn't imagine a guy who wouldn't want a woman like her on his arm.

"Here it is…." He tapped the notebook page before him as if he'd found what he was looking for. "This says you were embracing Mr. Capanna when the shot came. You were in his arms, he kissed you, then he was hit and you both fell to the sidewalk."

She closed her eyes but only for a second. "That *is* what happened."

"He was kissing you? But you'd just had him sign divorce papers?"

"We weren't going for each other's throats. It was a different kind of divorce."

"I didn't know there was another kind."

She didn't smile this time. "Kenneth wasn't happy about the situation but I'd convinced him a divorce was the best thing for both of us."

"Because?"

"Because it wasn't working out," she said. "We needed to move on. It was a mistake from the very beginning."

"Okay. I guess I can understand."

"I doubt that," she said. "But it doesn't matter, does it? He's gone. And you've got to figure out who did this."

Bishop turned the conversation in a different direction. "Do you have a list of his employees?"

"There was only one. Robin Estes, his assistant. I can give you her name and address if you like."

He copied down the information she recited. "I'll need access to his files."

"I can let you in the office. Just let me know when."

"I'd like to go as early as we can in the morning. Did you have anything to do with the company?"

She smiled briefly. "I bailed it out whenever he needed funds but that's about it. I'm no good when it comes to things like that."

"You must be good when it comes to your own work."

"Have you seen it?"

"No. But you support yourself and it looks like you did the same for him. I'd define that as success."

"I suppose you're right. I tend to define success differently than most people."

"How is that?"

"All I'm interested in is my art. If I'm able to create something that expresses the emotion I'm after then I've been successful."

"Tell me what you do."

Like before, it seemed as if she didn't want to answer him. Her expression shut down and she leaned back in her chair. He let the silence grow and wondered why she was so reluctant to discuss what she did.

"I build shadow boxes," she said finally.

Again he waited for an explanation. When the silence reached the awkward stage, she spoke once more.

"They're small boxes," she explained. "Glass on the front and sides, a tableau inside. They're…different."

He didn't force her. "And Sarah Levy sells them for you?"

"Yes."

She waited for more questions and he had them, but he wanted to get back to the scene and see if Carter had come up with anything. A quick glance at his watch told him how late it was.

He stood and tucked his notebook into his suit pocket. "We'll be talking again but I think we've covered enough tonight. In the meantime, don't forget my list." He paused. "Call your friends back and get them to stay with you. You've had a pretty traumatic evening."

"I've gone through worse by myself and made it to the other side." She looked out the darkened window behind him. "I'll do the same with this."

ANISE SHUT THE DOOR behind the cop, then rested her forehead against the wooden frame. She wanted to go to bed, to sleep and dream a senseless dream but she couldn't. She had to call Donna. As much as she disliked the woman, no one deserved to hear about the death of someone they once loved on the morning news.

She went to the desk in the living room and pulled the phone toward her. Her fingers felt numb as she dialed. When Donna answered, Anise tried to compare her voice to the person who'd called Kenneth earlier but the slurred "hello" didn't sound like the caller. It *was* two in the morning, though. Few people sounded like themselves when the phone rang at that time.

"Donna, this is Anise. Are you awake?"

"I am now. What the hell do you want? Do you know what time it is? For God's sake—"

That was typical Donna. Anise interrupted her tirade. "Donna, I have some bad news. I need you to listen to me."

"I'm listening."

"Kenneth's been shot. We met tonight to sign our divorce papers and when we walked out of the restaurant, someone… shot him."

Stunned silence echoed at Donna's end. "What is this? Are you kidding me? Is this some kinda sick joke like one of your sick pieces of art?"

"I'm telling you the truth." Anise closed her eyes and rubbed them with her thumb and forefinger. Starbursts formed in the blackness. "He's dead." She took a deep breath and the reality hit her all over again. "Kenneth's dead. He died in my arms in front of the restaurant."

Donna's gasp was loud, like fabric ripping. "He's dead... Are you sure?" Before Anise could answer, Donna asked a second question. "What time did this happen? Where were you?"

Her queries made no sense but few things Donna said ever did. "It was around seven or eight, I guess. I'm not sure. We were at Lido's—downtown."

She expected Donna to start crying but she didn't say a word. Anise wondered if she'd hung up. "Donna?"

Her answer was barely a whisper. "I'm here...."

"Can you tell Brittany?"

"Brittany…" She said her daughter's name as if it were a stranger's.

"Can you break the news to her?" Anise forged ahead with dogged determination. "She needs to hear it from you, not the TV or something. There might be reporters contacting you later. You don't want her to be blindsided."

She seemed to gather herself, although Anise couldn't really imagine that happening. "I'll talk to her," Donna promised. "I'll find her right now and tell her what happened."

Anise weighed the odds over whether or not Donna would follow through. Whatever they were, she couldn't worry about them now. She had enough to handle on her own. "I'll call you when I know more."

"I'll be waiting."

DESPITE HER PROMISE, Anise didn't call Sarah. She didn't have the emotional strength to fight with her friend and that's how the conversation would turn out because Anise didn't want her or Madelyn to come back. She wanted to be by herself and went straight to bed after talking to Donna even though she didn't expect to sleep. She dozed restlessly when things were going well. Tonight she'd do nothing but stare at the ceiling and replay the events of the day.

She closed her eyes and pretended regardless. Sometimes she could fool herself into a short nap.

It took less than a minute to realize that wasn't going to happen.

Behind her eyelids, the images came fast and furious, a slide show running amok. Everything that had happened from Kenneth easing into their booth on time to his final, dying gasp replayed itself behind her shuttered gaze. She tried to stop the visions from coming, but realized her efforts were pointless.

She got up, threw on her robe and went into her studio.

In the streetlight filtering through the windows everything looked just as it had earlier when she'd left to go meet Kenneth. The worktable was strewn with pieces of broken glass and lengths of wood. At her painting station by the window, brushes soaked in glass jars while tubes of paint littered the tabletop. Beside another window, her drawing easel stood ready. She'd half expected a tornado-like path of destruction to greet her.

She tightened her belt and walked slowly to her stool and the pad of paper propped up before it. Before she started a project she always sketched it out, the concept flowing from her brain to her fingertips without much conscious thought. She picked up the pencil and looked at it, her mind drifting back to her childhood. There had only been the two of them. Anise had no idea who her father was, and her mother hadn't had contact with her family for years. Mother and daughter had been incredibly close. Her mother had seen her talent early. When she'd hardly been able to feed them, she'd encouraged Anise with sets of colored pens and bordered papers. "Someday you'll be a famous artist," she'd predicted. "Your pretty pictures will hang everywhere—in fancy houses and important museums. You'll be legendary."

Anise hadn't known what legendary meant but from the shine in her mother's eyes when she made the pronouncement, Anise had known it was a good thing. Too bad her mother hadn't lived long enough to see part of her prediction come true. Anise was well-known in the art world and her pieces were displayed in "fancy houses." She wasn't legendary, though, and she didn't do "pretty pictures."

Any desire she might have had to do that had vanished the night her mother died. After she'd been pulled from the closet where she'd hidden, Anise had begun to see the universe differently than she had before. It had changed, just like the skin on her palms. It was full of danger and scary things and situations that could go wrong. If you weren't careful enough, you could die. People died every day. They left and you had to cope all by yourself.

From that point on, she'd been another person and no one, except Sarah, had even known she changed because no one else had known her that well before. She looked three times before she crossed the street. She wore a cross *and* the Star of David. She guarded her emotions and her body and most of all her heart. That's why she'd married Kenneth. She hadn't loved him so she'd thought it might be safe. Her plan had worked for a while, but then she'd come to care for him. In return, he'd wanted more of her and she hadn't been able to give it to him. Now he was gone, too.

She sat down on the stool, with only the streetlight for illumination. A pattern of leaves from the pin oak danced across the tablet before her and her pencil drifted over the paper trying to catch the design.

When the sun came up, she was still drawing. The doorbell brought her out of the trance and her eyes shot to the clock that hung between the windows on her right. It was seven.

BISHOP STARTED TO CURSE. He'd told her he would call first but he hadn't had the time; now he was standing on Anise's front porch with ten dollars' worth of fancy coffee and she wasn't answering her door.

He'd left last night with the impression she wanted to be by herself but maybe she'd changed her mind—or her friends had changed it for her—and she'd gone to spend the night with them after all. He wouldn't have wanted to be alone if he had gone through what she had. But a moment later, the door swung open.

She wore the same thick robe she'd had on before, her hair pulled back from her face, no makeup on her skin. Nothing was different about her but she looked smaller in the morning light, less in control. Her expression was startled—she'd clearly forgotten he was coming over.

"I'm sorry I didn't phone first," he said. "I got busy. But I did bring coffee…."

"No…no, it's fine." She looked at the Starbucks cups in his hand and held her door open wider. He stepped inside the house he'd left only a few hours earlier and handed her one of the coffees.

"You didn't have to do that," she said. "But thank you anyway."

"I thought you could use the extra caffeine."

"I never went to sleep," she said. "So I didn't have to wake up."

He understood now. "I can come back later if you're not ready."

"No, that's not necessary." She smoothed her free hand down her ponytail. "If you don't mind waiting, I can be ready in ten minutes. I know you need to get into Kenneth's office."

Once again, she managed to surprise him. He would have taken her for a woman who needed hours to get dressed. It took his ex ten minutes to even *prepare* her face to put on her makeup.

"That would really be great," he said.

"I can't be gone all day," she warned. "I have a lot to do."

"Ms. Estes can drive you back. I want us to ride together so I can tell you on the way about the headway we've made."

Her eyes opened wide. "Did you cat—"

"No, nothing like that," he said. "But we've gotten a few leads."

She spoke over her shoulder as she left the room. "I won't be long. Make yourself at home."

He'd been hoping she'd say something like that.

Sipping his coffee, he looked around the living room he'd only passed through the night before. The area was nicely decorated but it could have been a hotel lobby. It didn't seem lived-in. There were no personal photos or travel mementoes or knickknacks of the sort people usually picked up during a lifetime. Hoping to learn more about who Anise really was, he made quick work of the kitchen and dining room, then headed down the hallway that went the opposite direction from her bedroom. From outside he'd guessed it was her studio and when he stepped inside, he saw he'd been right.

He realized something else as well. The rest of the house served its purpose but here was where she really existed.

Windows lined every wall. In the past this had been someone's sunroom, a place to retreat and view the garden and sip iced tea. The comfortable couches and hooked rugs he imagined were long gone, though. Brick pavers lined the floor and worktables filled the space. He took another sip of coffee and walked to the nearest one. It was covered with scraps of wood and fabric. A tiny plastic doll was propped up at one end, a miniature snake lying beside her. He stared at the bits and pieces and wondered how it all went together. Then something on one of the other tables caught his eye. He put down his cup and crossed the space to look.

It was a shallow glass box, about ten inches wide and twelve long. The lid, also made of glass and framed in wood, was smeared with something that obscured the contents.

He lifted the top and peered inside. Lined in red velvet, the box held a collection of tiny objects, none bigger than his thumb, dividers creating three distinct areas. One part held a diminutive bed with a tiny painted chest beside it, one held a small black table, and in the third sat a piece of paper cut like a heart with a ragged slash running down the length of it. It looked like a Valentine, the kind that kids made and gave to each other. Each of the items had been placed precisely but other things had the look of being tossed in. A doll's tennis shoe, the eraser from a pencil, a glittering sequin…

None of it made sense to Bishop. But he *was* fascinated by it. And that's why he didn't hear Anise when she walked into the room.

CHAPTER FOUR

"WHAT ARE YOU DOING?"

Bishop turned as Anise spoke. She didn't appreciate his presence in her studio and she wasn't bothering to hide it.

"What are you doing in here?" she repeated.

"My job," he said.

"Snooping in here won't help you find Kenneth's killer."

"You never know," he answered. "Sometimes things you think aren't important turn out to be significant in a case like this. I have to get all the information then decide."

His words didn't seem to mollify her but he continued before she could say more. "Tell me about this." He waved a hand toward the box. "What does it represent?"

"I don't talk about my work." Her words

came out stiff. As if realizing how harsh she'd sounded, she tried again. "You know artists...they're funny about stuff like that."

"Actually I don't know any artists," he said. "So enlighten me."

"It's like a jinx, I guess. If I tell you what it's all about, then it won't come out right." She took a piece of black silk from the table and draped it over the box, a phone starting to ring as she did so. She stepped to the desk in one corner of the room and answered.

The person on the other end of the line was angry. Bishop could hear the agitated voice from where he stood. When the caller paused, Anise spoke into the silence.

"I'm sorry, Sarah. I know I promised."

The art dealer continued her harangue and Bishop began to understand. Anise hadn't called her friend back. He wasn't surprised by her reaction. Sarah Levy had grated on his nerves the night before but he also appreciated the fact that she wanted to protect her friend. He didn't run across that too much anymore. People never seemed to put anyone else first.

"Yes, it was wrong..." More talk. "I'm

sure you *were* worried, yes…" Anise let the other woman continue then finally, she raised her hand. "Look, Sarah, I'm sorry I upset you, okay? It *was* thoughtless and I won't do it again, but I was tired and I thought you'd understand."

The voice on the other end dropped and became conciliatory and Anise responded in kind. "No, no, it's okay. But I can't talk right now. I've got to go to Kenneth's office with the investigator. He needs to examine the files and talk to Robin. I'll call you later, okay?" A pause. "I *will* phone, I promise. I'm writing myself a note right now, okay? Good…bye-bye."

She hung up the phone and turned, a sheepish expression on her face. "I didn't call my friend last night."

"Seems like she didn't cut you any slack, either."

"Sarah doesn't know how to do that for anyone, including herself." She smiled, then the expression slipped away. "I was just so out of it… All I wanted to do was work…."

"I'm sure she understood once you explained. I would."

Her eyes met his and she lifted an eyebrow as if to ask why.

"Let's just say, I have some experience in that area myself. Sometimes it's easier to concentrate on work than to deal with the hard stuff."

"The hard stuff being?"

He answered truthfully. It was the only way he knew how. "The hard stuff being life," he said. "Nothing about it is easy. Not as far as I can see."

TEN MINUTES LATER they were in Bishop's car, heading for Kenneth's office. The freeway was a mess as usual, the ever-present construction a daily occurrence for Houston drivers. They merged on I10 at a crawl then slowed down even further, all the lanes that ran downtown at a virtual standstill.

Anise turned to the cop sitting beside her. Finding him in her studio then getting Sarah's call had flustered her but she didn't want him to know that. She wasn't sure why. Generally speaking, she didn't care what people thought about her yet for some reason she wanted to impress him.

"Tell me what you learned," she asked in an attempt to regain her bearings. "You said you'd found something?"

He glanced over his shoulder and bullied his way into another lane. "One of the kids who works the valet stand at the restaurant saw a guy running down a side street right after the shooting. He couldn't see much beyond that, though. The runner had on a sweatshirt with a hood and it was pulled up to hide his face. We're following up on that. If he saw him, then someone else probably saw him, too."

She caught her breath. "Do you think it was the person who shot Kenneth?"

"I have no way of knowing." His hands went tight on the steering wheel. "But I'm damn sure gonna try and find him so I can ask him that question myself."

She nodded and looked out the window, her stomach in knots.

"Something else came up when I went back to the scene."

She turned to stare at the detective's

profile again. The car they were in was a big one but he seemed to fill up more than his share of the front seat. "What?"

Instead of answering her question, he asked her another one. "Did your husband have a girlfriend?"

"Not that I knew about," she said. "But I wouldn't be surprised."

He cut in front of a delivery truck and gained them an extra five feet before shooting her a glance. "Why is that?"

"Kenneth was a nice-looking man. He wouldn't have been lonely for long."

"The idea doesn't disturb you? I mean, your divorce wasn't final, was it? Some women might not like that."

"At this point in the game, I hardly think it matters."

"Not even to your ego?"

"I don't have an ego. I'm not famous enough."

"I'm not famous, period, but I wouldn't appreciate my wife hooking up with someone else."

She hesitated. She'd had her suspicions but she'd never confronted Kenneth so she wasn't sure. Finally she answered. "If he'd had someone when we still cared for each other, that would have bothered me, I suppose. But he'd moved out and I'd moved on."

"Do you have someone new?"

The question was so ludicrous, Anise almost laughed. At the last minute she managed to catch herself. "I'm too involved with my work. I don't have time for anyone else and even if I did, I wouldn't be interested."

"Why?"

"I'm happy being alone. I should never have married Kenneth in the first place. It was a big mistake for me and an even bigger one for him."

ROBIN ESTES WAS WAITING for them when they reached the office. She was one of those small, mousy women no one ever really saw. Medium height, medium build, medium everything. The only distinguishing thing about her was her nervousness and even that seemed ordinary. Cops tended to make people feel that way.

She jumped up from her desk and rushed to Anise as they walked inside. "Oh, Anise, I can't believe what happened! I was so shocked last night."

Anise let the woman run on, her platitudes the usual ones. When she paused to take a breath, Anise introduced her to Bishop. "We're here so Investigator Bishop can look at the files, Robin. He needs to see what Kenneth was working on."

He shook her hand and tried not to intimidate her but apparently he failed. Her eyes grew large.

"I'll need to know more about all Mr. Capanna's clients but I'm especially interested in the woman he told Anise about last night. The one with the IRS problems."

The secretary blinked rapidly, shooting Anise a frightened look. "Who was Kenneth talking about?"

"I don't know. He didn't give me a name. He just said someone had been calling and threatening him but he didn't think she was serious. He didn't seem concerned."

Her brown hair hanging in her eyes, Robin shook her head. "I—I don't know who he meant. We don't have anyone under audit right now."

"Are you sure?" Bishop smiled encouragingly. "It would really help—"

She glared at him, her attitude going from anxious to arrogant. "I'm familiar with every client we have and I can assure you there are no cases like that in this office."

Bishop held up his hands. "I understand. Maybe you could just show me the most recent ones, then. We'll start there. I'll glance over them while you take Ms. Borden home. By the time you get back, I may have some questions for you."

Her eyes darted to Anise as if seeking permission. Anise gave it, repeating the words he'd said to her earlier in her studio. "We need to show him everything, Robin. The more information Bishop has, the better his chances are of catching Kenneth's killer."

She scurried out of the reception area and headed for Capanna's office.

Bishop turned to Anise. "I almost forgot…I spoke with Donna Capanna early this morning and she told me about your conversation last night. Thank you for calling her."

"It wasn't a problem."

"Good. In the meantime, I'd appreciate it if you'd keep close. If you have to go out of town, let me know first."

In the silence that followed, she stared at him in surprise. Bishop doubted that Anise Borden had anything to do with Kenneth Capanna's murder but he'd seen women who looked more innocent than her turn out to blood-thirsty killers. Anything was possible.

"This is standard in these kinds of cases," he explained. "We always look at the family. Don't take offense."

"But I...I was standing right next to him! How could I have shot him?"

"Killings for hire happen more than you realize."

A silence charged with animosity flared between them. "I won't be going anywhere," she said stiffly.

"That's fine. And I'd like you to think about what I said earlier, too. If Kenneth was seeing someone, I need a name."

"If I had one, I'd give it to you."

"Maybe something will come to you."

"I doubt that."

"You never know."

They looked at each other under the harsh lights and Bishop realized he was having a hard time reading the woman before him. It was a skill that usually came second nature to him but Anise was an enigma, just like the boxes she created. In the other room, a metal drawer slammed shut then Robin Estes returned, at least a dozen files in her arms. She didn't look like she wanted to turn them over. "These cover everyone we have under contract right now. Don't you need a warrant or something, though?"

"That's not necessary since I have Ms. Borden's permission."

Anise kept her eyes on Bishop's face. "Give him the files, Robin, then let's go. The investigator needs to do his job."

Placing the files on the desk, Robin retrieved her purse and started for the door. As Anise followed, Bishop put his hand on her arm and stopped her.

"I want to know what the box in your studio represents," he said. "You can tell me because I don't believe in jinxes. For a curse to work, you have to believe and I don't."

When she didn't reply, he pressed her. "I want to understand what you're trying to express."

"So do I," she said in a cool voice. "If I figure it out, I'll tell you."

ROBIN RAMBLED all the way back to Anise's house, her disjointed conversation full of conjecture over what might have happened to Kenneth. She was always nervous and flighty but today she seemed worse than usual. Anise made the appropriate sounds at the right time (or so she hoped) but she focused more on what Bishop had hinted at before she'd left the office.

He suspected her?

The idea was so ridiculous she hadn't even understood him at first. She and Kenneth could have had a better marriage but to even suggest Anise could do something like that was beyond the pale. And to what end? There was no money involved and he'd agreed to give her the divorce. Why would she have even wanted him dead? She cursed under her breath, wishing she'd come up with those arguments at the time.

Which made her remember Bishop's other surprise, the query about Kenneth and a girlfriend.

His question had presented the perfect opening to explain that in the back of her mind she *had* suspected Kenneth had a girlfriend yet something had stopped her from acknowledging that fact. As stupid as it was, she supposed that something was her pride, despite what she'd told the detective earlier. She hadn't wanted to tell him what she'd noticed but done nothing about. Kenneth had been frequently absent from his office, though, and more than once she'd answered the phone at home only to have the person at the other end hang up when they heard her voice. There had been charges on the credit card bill she hadn't understood, and once she'd found a folded napkin in the pocket of his coat. It'd had the name of a Chinese restaurant printed on it. One they'd never visited, at least not together.

Robin jerked to a stop in front of Anise's house. "Would you like me to come in? I can stay awhile if you want or—"

"I think you better get back to the office," Anise suggested. "The investigator might have some questions."

"Oh, yeah, well…okay, then. Call me if you need anything."

"I will." Anise got out of the car, but Robin called her name just as she was about to slam the door.

"What about the office?" Robin asked. "Should I keep it open or what?"

A flash of resentment came then left. Anise didn't want to be the person who handled Kenneth's affairs, but who else was going to do it? Donna wasn't capable of such a thing even if she'd wanted to help. She had never worked and she knew even less about Kenneth's business than Anise.

Anise thought for a moment, then she remembered an attorney Kenneth had consulted on several different occasions. "Keep it open for now," she replied. "I'll contact Robert Siha and have him look over the pending cases. When he finishes, wrap up the ones you can then send letters to the others explaining the office will be closing. I'll decide when later. Can you handle that for me?"

"No problem." Robin nodded her head vigorously. She liked to receive direction, which was one of the reasons she and Sarah got along so well. "I guess I need to look for another job, too."

"That would probably be a good idea."

Anise told Robin goodbye then headed up the path. When she opened the front door, the phone was ringing.

And it continued to ring the rest of the morning. The press had managed to get her phone number and every television station in town wanted her comment. She tried, without success, to reach Sarah, then turned the phone off, the reporters' ghoulish questions too much to handle.

At noon, when someone knocked on the door, she had no intention of answering it. Her curiosity got the better of her, however, and she found herself peering out the window in the entry. Madelyn and Sarah stood on the porch, each woman holding two bags from a deli down the street.

"We brought lunch," Madelyn announced as Anise opened the door, "so don't even try and say you're not hungry. You're going to eat, regardless."

They bustled inside and went straight to the kitchen, Sarah pulling out the plates and glasses, Madelyn finding the napkins and silverware. Each woman knew the others' kitchens as well as her own.

Anise didn't argue. Turning her phone back on, she sat down at the table in her breakfast nook and watched them.

"How did it go at the office?" Sarah put a pickle on each plate as she spoke. "Can Robin handle things there?"

"Fine and yes," Anise answered. "I told her to start wrapping things up and she said she would."

Madelyn divided the sandwiches and potato salad then looked up, her eyes warm. "And how are you doing?"

"I'll be okay." Anise lined up the salt and pepper shakers with the sugar bowl that sat on the table. "But I'm supposed to think about whether or not Kenneth had a girlfriend and I can't go anywhere."

Sarah's head jerked up. "What? Who says you can't go anywhere?"

Anise explained.

"That's outrageous," Sarah snapped. "The man can't possibly think you had anything to do with this. You need to get yourself a lawyer, Anise. I'm calling—"

"You're not calling anyone," Anise said sharply. "He has a point. Just settle down and let him do his thing."

"I didn't like his attitude last night. I should have known better and stayed here. You can't stand by and let him railroad you like this!"

"Sarah, for God's sake, he's not railroading anyone." Defending Bishop put Anise in an odd position, making her see his point of view. The animosity she'd felt toward him earlier vanished. "He's only doing his job."

Madelyn picked up two of the plates and brought them to the table. "You two need to give it a break. We're going to have lunch like civilized people and put this on the back burner at least while we eat."

Madelyn was right, as she always was. With an expression of contrition, Sarah sat down beside Anise, who held out her hand and squeezed her fingers. They each managed one bite from their sandwiches when the phone rang.

Anise was out of her chair before it could ring again. "I am *not* making any statements to the press," she said into the receiver, "so you people can just stop calling!"

"I'm not with the press," the businesslike voice said at the other end of the line. "My name is Leslie Sandoval and I'm with the Harris County Medical Examiner's Office. Am I speaking with Anise Borden?"

Anise drew in sharp breath. "Ye...yes."

"You were listed as Mr. Kenneth Capanna's next of kin. I'm calling to inform you our autopsy is finished and we're ready to release the body. What would you like to do?"

CHAPTER FIVE

SHE WASN'T PREPARED for the question but Anise didn't have a choice. It hung in the air until she named a funeral home a half block from her house. The place came to mind only because she passed the graceful brick facade every time she went to the grocery store.

"We'll take care of it," the woman promised. "You'll need to call them later and make your arrangements."

Anise promised she would, then she hung up and explained the call to Madelyn and Sarah.

"Good grief." Sarah dropped her sandwich back to her plate. "Why on earth do you have to deal with that? Can't someone else handle it?"

"Kenneth was an only child. Both his

parents are dead. Donna would only mess it up." Anise took a breath. "Since we were still officially married when he died, I guess I'm it."

With somber looks, they finished their lunch and reluctantly left Anise alone once more.

She didn't prolong her duty. She phoned the funeral director and told him what to do. Then she called Robert Siha. As soon as she finished with the attorney, who agreed to help wrap up Kenneth's cases for a reasonable fee, she dialed Donna's number. Regardless of what Anise did, Donna would be unhappy with the plans so Anise wanted to get the disclosure behind her. She'd made the arrangements without consulting her and Donna was just going to have to live with them.

"How dare you do this without talking to me?" Sure enough, Donna was indignant.

"It's what Kenneth wanted," Anise said. "He told me so himself. No service. No announcements. Just a cremation."

"I don't believe you," Donna retorted.

If she'd been Donna, Anise wouldn't

have believed it, either, but she and
Kenneth had discussed the situation once
and he'd made himself clear. She'd remembered because it had seemed so out of
character for him. She would have
expected him to want a big affair to mark
his passing on.

"I'm sorry, Donna, but it's a done deal.
I've already taken care of everything."

"Then we'll have a memorial here at the
house. Tomorrow evening. I insist."

"I can't stop you," Anise said. "If that's
what you want to do, feel free."

Anise's acquiescence clearly took
Donna by surprise; the anger left her
voice and she replaced it with uncertainty.
"Will you come?"

Her question—and the tone in which she
asked it—also caught Anise off guard. "Of
course I'll come," she said.

"I think you should," the other woman
said. "It's the proper thing to do."

"You're right," Anise replied. "It is. Just
let me know what time."

"I'll call the caterer as soon as I get off
the phone."

Anise said her goodbye then left the phone sitting off the hook once again. She headed for her studio. No more conversations. No more decisions.

She'd had enough.

She entered her studio and went to the drawing she'd been working on when Bishop had arrived that morning. He'd been right. The hard stuff *was* life and she couldn't face another minute of it for now.

DONNA CAPANNA'S HOUSE occupied a corner lot smack in the middle of Bunker Hill Village. The community was one of half a dozen small enclaves that Houston had grown up around but it maintained its own government. Another point of difference existed between it and Houston as well. The median family income for the thirty-six hundred people who lived inside its limits was $200,000.

The homes were huge, the crime rate low and the citizens rich.

Bishop parked the Crown Vic behind a long line of Mercedes, Beemers and Volvos filling up both sides of the street and made his way to the house. A Hispanic woman wearing a starched white uniform opened the door and nodded toward the living room. "Welcome," she said. "The family is in there."

He wondered which family she meant as he crossed the elegant foyer, the patterned rug thick beneath his shoes. A moment later, he had his answer.

Accepting condolences with the grace of a queen, an overblown blonde sat on a couch situated in front of a large bay window. She wore black and held a lace-edge handkerchief. An older couple, her parents he presumed, was sitting on either side of her, each taking turns patting her arm. If the camera had been rolling, she would have been ready for her close-up.

He went over and held out his hand, his words drawing the glance of everyone near enough to hear. "Mrs. Capanna? I'm Daniel Bishop with HPD. Homicide. We spoke on the phone. I'm investigating Mr. Capanna's murder."

Fresh tears sprang into her eyes. "Oh,

yes… Thank you so much for coming. Are you making any progress?"

Her words sounded as scripted as the setting.

"We're doing all that we can," he said.

"I'm sure you are." She dabbed at her eyes then waved the handkerchief. "Please help yourself to a drink and some food. We'll talk more later."

"That sounds fine. Thank you."

Playing his part, he stepped back and let the next mourner take his place. He shook his head mentally. He'd come from a large Scotch-Irish clan. When somebody died in his family, the affairs that followed were noisy and confused, kids running around with food in their hands, someone yelling, someone else fighting. He reminded himself again that diversity was good but the stifled formality set his teeth on edge.

Then he heard a raised voice. It dropped immediately, but a moment later he heard it again. His curiosity aroused, he found himself wandering down a hallway. The farther he went, the louder the voices became. An argument! Thank God…

"This is all your fault!" He heard a young girl's words, strained and angry. "If you hadn't married my dad, he'd be alive right now!"

"Brittany, you're not making sense. Please calm down and think about what you're saying. How on earth—"

Bishop recognized Anise's calm tones. The girl had to be Capanna's teenaged daughter.

"I *am* thinking about it and it *does* make sense. You took him away from me and my mom. Otherwise we'd *still* be a family. And we'd *still* be happy. He wouldn't have been meeting you at that stupid restaurant and he'd *still* be alive!"

"Your parents were divorced a long time before your dad and I met, Brittany. You know that."

"They were going to get back together. My mom told me so. They were going to remarry then you came along and broke them up!"

"That's not what happened—"

"Yes, it is! Don't lie! I know it was the

truth! Otherwise they wouldn't have been going to remarry now!"

"What on earth are you talking about?"

"They were going to get married again as soon as you let him go! The minute the divorce was final, my dad was coming back to us. Mom said so!"

Bishop froze. If Brittany Capanna had her story straight, he had to look at the case in a completely different way. *Could* her mother and father have been reconciling? Bishop filled in the blanks, his mind grabbing the idea and considering all the possibilities.

"Brittany, your mother wasn't telling you the truth if that's what she said." Anise's voice was tinged with shock. "Are you sure you understood her correctly?"

"I understood exactly what she meant, dammit—"

"I don't think so—"

"You're the one who's lying!" The girl screamed her accusation, reaching a point of hysteria. "You tried to make me think you wanted to be my friend, but that wasn't the truth, either. My mother always told me you were a bitch and now I know she was right—"

"Brittany—"

Bishop reached the doorway at the same time the teenaged girl shot from the room. Taller than he expected and cigarette-skinny, she had hazel eyes and unnaturally black hair, a gold ring piercing each eyebrow. She crashed into his chest with a thud, cried out then stumbled. She would have gone down but Bishop managed to catch her arms and keep the poor kid upright. "Whoa, there…" he cried. "Are you okay?"

Her startled eyes connected with his, then she fled, a trail of angry sobs echoing behind her.

Anise stood on the threshold and stared at Bishop, her mouth hanging open in surprise.

"What's going on? Are you all right?" he asked.

"I can't believe…" She threw a glance down the hallway, but the teenager was long gone. She'd hit Bishop like a running back heading down the sideline, the end zone in view.

"Did you hear what she said?" Anise asked.

He took Anise by the elbow and guided her back into the room. Her skin was warm and smooth beneath his fingers and he had to remind himself of who she was. Getting interested in a victim's widow was the last thing Bishop needed. If his boss found out Bishop was even having thoughts in that direction, he'd yank him off the case and send his ass back to patrol. Not a place Bishop wanted to be.

But she sure smelled good.

"Yes, I did." He focused on her question. "Is it true?"

She blinked and her lips parted again. "No, it's not true! Kenneth wasn't going back to Donna. He would have shot *himself* before he did that! She's crazy! Didn't you see her out there?"

"I saw her," he said, "but that's not the point. If Mr. Capanna was planning on returning to his first wife, it puts a different spin on his murder."

A frown furrowed her forehead, but then she seemed to puzzle his meaning out.

"That's insane," Anise whispered. "He was not going back to Donna. No way. I was the one who wanted the divorce, not Kenneth."

"And who knew that besides you?"

"Sarah," she said. "And Madelyn."

"Your best friends?"

"Yes," she said, "but if you don't believe me, then ask my lawyer. I can call him right now and ask him to tell you the truth."

"That would be fine," he said. "I appreciate the effort but don't bother."

Her eyes filled with confusion. "Wh-why not?"

"He's *your* attorney. All he cares about is you. If he said anything other than what you just told me, I'd tell you to fire him. It's his job to protect you."

"But it's the truth."

"Truth is relative," he said. "Ask Brittany if you don't believe me."

A beam of sunshine came through the window behind them and motes danced in the light. Anise Borden didn't seem capable of planning a murder but he had to consider every angle. And this was one he hadn't thought of before now.

THEY WENT BACK into the living room, Anise's legs were so shaky she wasn't sure she could make it to a chair. Bishop's words had left her confused and anxious yet the concern on his face when he'd seen Brittany's distress was an image she couldn't forget, either. Sarah appeared as Anise sat down.

"You look pale. Did he say something to you?" Sarah sent the detective a hostile glare, then turned to Robin, who had wandered up. "Go get her some food and something to drink."

"I'm fine. And I can get my own plate—"

Both women ignored her protests, Robin taking off to do Sarah's biding, Sarah insisting to know more.

"What happened?" she demanded.

"Nothing," Anise said, "I'm a little upset."

"Why is that?"

Anise explained Brittany's attack but held back the details of her conversation with Bishop. It would make Sarah angry and it didn't mean anything regardless. Bishop couldn't possibly think she had engineered Kenneth's murder—it was just a ploy. Something to make her think a little harder about who might be responsible.

"I don't trust him," Sarah said darkly. "I saw him in the kitchen and he asked if he could come by the studio tomorrow. Cops are one step away from being criminals themselves, you know."

Robin reappeared with a plate of tea sandwiches and fresh fruit salad in one hand, a cup of coffee in the other. She handed them to Anise.

"That's ridiculous," Anise said. "He's doing his job, Sarah. He has to ask hard questions."

"He wasn't that bad when I talked to him." Robin fiddled nervously with one of the buttons on her jacket. Her fingernails had been chewed to the quick. "You know, when he was at the office?"

"What did he ask you?" Anise tried to seem casual.

"Where I was that night and stuff like

that." Robin nibbled at one corner of her mouth, her lipstick long gone. "Sarah and I were together, remember? We saw the police lights and went down to the restaurant and Kenneth was lying there—"

Always the protective one, Sarah cut her friend off with a wave of her hand. "Anise doesn't need a replay, Robin. She remembers."

Robin nodded, her face turning red. "Oh, jeez… I'm sorry, Anise."

Before Anise could reply, Madelyn joined the group, juggling a plate and drink. She threw a quick look over her shoulder, then turned back and made a face at them.

"I can't believe how Donna is acting. It's a bit much, isn't it? Even for her?"

Glancing toward the couch, Robin and Sarah murmured their agreement but Anise's attention was pulled past the spot where Donna was still enthroned. She stared instead at a willowy Asian woman waiting near the door. She would have stood out in any crowd but she looked like some kind of exotic bird, her bright pink dress and matching lipstick adding an unexpected splash of color among the group of darkly dressed mourners.

"Who is that woman?" Anise murmured. "The one by the front door? In the fuchsia dress?"

Robin looked over her shoulder, then, as if looking for an answer herself, glanced at Madelyn. Sarah spoke before Madelyn could say a word. "I don't know," she said. "Probably some friend of Donna's." She pointed to Anise's plate. "Would you please eat your sandwiches? You've barely touched your plate. You can't afford to lose any weight!"

Anise smiled and shook her head. "Talk about a Jewish mother!"

"You need one," Madelyn jumped in. "And she's right. You have to eat." The three women formed a cordon around her and Anise was trapped. Fifteen minutes later, the plate was empty and the crowd had begun to thin as well.

Sarah took Anise's plate then handed it to Robin who headed for the kitchen. "We're leaving when Robin comes back," she announced. "We can all go out together."

Sarah nodded, her eyes searching the crowd once more. Bishop was nowhere to be seen and the woman in the pink dress was gone as well. They said their goodbyes to Donna and slipped out a moment later.

Thirty minutes after that, Sarah's Jeep pulled up in front of Anise's house. The four women got out and stood under the pin oak that filled Anise's front yard with shade.

Madelyn did her motherly thing. "Are you sure you wouldn't like one of us to stay with you, Anise?"

"I don't need a babysitter. I'm fine, really."

"You may think you're fine," Sarah said, "but seeing Ken gunned down like that is bound to affect you, sweetheart. Visions like that can't just be forgotten. It would be okay to need us, you know."

"You're right, Sarah, and you're kind, Madelyn, but I just want to be by myself. I handle things better that way. I always have."

"We understand, but you don't have to do *this* alone." Sarah squeezed her shoulder. "We're here."

"And I'm glad," Anise said. "But I want to work. That will make me feel better than anything else. I want to concentrate on my pieces for the show."

They'd been planning the event for a good two months, building a cocktail party around a dozen new boxes that Anise was creating. Invitation only. Champagne and hors d'oeuvres. Anise hadn't been enthusiastic because it meant she would have to put in an appearance and make small talk, something she detested, but Sarah had said it was time. They needed to take her to a different level.

"Oh, my, I forgot all about the show," Madelyn said. "It's in a couple of weeks, isn't it?"

Sarah nodded. "I sent out the invitations last Monday." She turned to Anise. "We could reschedule it, though, if you'd rather not—"

"No. Don't change the date. I'm depending on it." Anise paused. "I *have* to do it."

Sarah patted her on the back, then gave her a quick hug. "I knew you'd say that. We'll leave you alone but call me tonight, okay?"

"I will."

ANISE AND HER FRIENDS had been gone for twenty minutes. The house was almost empty of people. Timing his approach, Bishop waited for the older couple to abandon Donna Capanna then he slipped into the man's spot on the couch. Donna couldn't escape and her expression told him she wasn't happy about that fact, especially since her audience was gone.

"Have you got a moment?" he asked with a smile.

"Is it really necessary? I'm exhausted. I'm sure you understand—"

"I won't take long," he said. "I just wanted to go over a few things with you."

"Such as?"

"Such as your guests today. I'd like to see a list of them."

Her arched eyebrows went up a notch. "Why is that?"

"It's standard procedure," he said, repeating his catch-all phrase. "Just to see if a name jumps out."

"All right," she said. "I'll see that you get it. What else?"

"Your daughter—"

"What about Brittany?" she asked sharply.

"I overheard her telling someone that you and Mr. Capanna were planning a reconciliation. Is this true?"

She blushed under her makeup and he had his answer. She'd lied to her daughter but why? "Who did she tell that to?"

"I didn't know them," he lied as well.

"Well, what possible difference could that make on your investigation?"

"Probably none," he said. "But I like to keep my ducks lined up. You know, standard—"

"Procedure." She filled in the word for him, her expression skeptical.

He waited for her answer but it didn't come. He prodded her. "Was it true?"

"Brittany's a difficult child." She pulled on the jacket of her suit, straightening it. "She wanted her father back at home."

"That doesn't answer my question."

"Anise Borden stole him from our family," she countered. "We were very happy together and having him here again would have been much better for everyone involved." She dabbed at her eyes. "Now that's not going to happen."

Trying to get a truthful answer from this woman was a waste of time. He switched topics. "You told me when we spoke earlier that you were with your parents the night Mr. Capanna was shot. I was just wondering…was your daughter with you that evening?"

She blinked. "Yes. Of course, she was."

"And you were at their home?"

"Yes. We were having dinner. Broiled salmon, asparagus—"

Interrupting her, he smiled. "I don't have to know the menu. But I would like to speak with Brittany at some point. You'll need to sign a consent form for that."

"And if I don't?"

"Then it gets complicated." He spoke politely as he stood. "There's no reason you should mind her speaking with me, Mrs. Capanna. If she was with you as you say, I won't have much to ask her."

"I'll think about it. She's been traumatized by her father's murder. I don't want to do anything that would upset her even more."

"Of course." He headed for the foyer, pausing at the doorway. "One last thing," he said.

She sighed. "Yes?"

"I noticed an Asian woman here, bright pink dress, very attractive. Who was she?"

"I have no idea." She frowned. "She might have been a client of Kenneth's. I instructed Robin Estes to make sure all of them knew about the gathering. You should ask her about the woman."

"I will. But I was hoping you might know her as well."

"I have no idea who she was," Donna said in a dismissive manner. "She could have wandered in from the street for all I know."

Bishop stared in silence at the woman seated on the couch. Though he had no reason to, he compared her to Anise Borden.

There was no contest.

It was a little past midnight when the doorbell rang.

Anise looked up, her tweezers poised above the box she was working on, a miniature tree made of black plastic caught in their grip. Who on earth could it be? It was too late for reporters and she wasn't expecting anyone. Hesitating, she waited for a second. Then when the sound wasn't repeated, she pretended she hadn't heard it in the first place.

Staring through the lighted magnifying glass she kept attached to her table, Anise placed the tree into the box, laying it upside down, her touch precise, the image in her mind unfolding before her. The title of this piece was *Green*. Everything inside it was black. She wasn't sure where she was going with it, but she liked where it was headed.

The doorbell rang again.

She placed her tweezers on the table, then walked to the row of windows that faced the street. Sometimes she could see who was at her door if they were standing in the right place. Pulling aside the shade on the nearest window, she peered out into the darkness.

Nothing moved except the leaves on the oak. Even the street was empty.

She stared a second longer then dropped

the shade. A reporter would have a car. A neighbor would have called first, especially this late. She was trying to decide what to do when the bell rang a third time. A sweep of alarm she couldn't explain rushed through her at the sound.

Moving as quietly as she could down the hallway, she entered the foyer and paused at the door, peeling back the curtains to look out the side window.

The porch was empty.

She frowned and started to open the door to step outside and look. A second thought held her still, though, her fingers freezing on the doorknob.

She'd heard about thieves who read obituary notices posted in the paper. They'd note the time of the services for the deceased then break in while everyone was gone. Someone obviously wanted to see if she was home but didn't want to be seen. Anyone who'd overheard Sarah or Madelyn beg her to stay with them might assume she'd done so tonight....

Bishop's face popped into her mind. She could call him. Something told her he would be there in minutes but what would she say to him once he'd arrived?

Someone rang my doorbell and I got scared...?

How lame was that?

She closed her eyes against the thought and forced it away but as soon as she did so, another one, equally unwanted, replaced it. Whoever had called Kenneth the night he'd been shot had not been happy. If she had his phone number, did she know where he'd lived? He had only moved out a month before. Not that long. Anise had no reason to think she could be the next target but who knew?

Her mouth went dry as the possibilities ran through her mind.

A scratching broke the silence. It had come from the porch. Her heart thumping erratically, she forced herself back to the window. Lifting the curtain with a single finger, she stared outside again.

A leaf danced across the steps then disappeared into the night. The street was just as empty as before. She let the curtain drop and went back to work.

CHAPTER SIX

THE REPORTS WERE piling up. It was Monday morning and Bishop hadn't been to his office since he'd pulled the Capanna case. He dropped his briefcase on the floor beside his desk then sat down in his squeaky chair, his eyes going to the folder on the top of the stack.

It was the book on Capanna. Carter had been a busy boy while Bishop had been out. He pushed the rest of the pile to one side and opened the notebook to see what progress the rookie had made. Thumbing through the pages, Bishop scanned the autopsy report (Capanna had taken one shot from a forty-five to the head), the witness notes (other than the valet no one saw anything) and numerous other bits and pieces of information connected to the dead lawyer (he owed MasterCard $8595.46 and three other credit cards equal or greater amounts). It appeared that Capanna had been a busy boy, too.

When he finished, Bishop started at the beginning and went over everything again. Raising his head an hour later, he cursed when he realized how much time had passed. He was going to be late to see Levy and something told him that wasn't good. She didn't look like she had much tolerance for anything, much less a tardy cop.

He walked the few blocks that separated the gallery from the cop shop, thinking about what he'd learned in the reports. One thing was clear: the killing had not been a professional hit. Pros didn't use forty-fives. A rifle shot from the nearest skyscraper would have been much cleaner and much easier. Anise Borden—or anyone else for that matter—had not ordered a hit on Kenneth Capanna.

When he stepped inside Levy's, footsteps greeted him. To his surprise, Anise appeared, a handbag over one shoulder, an empty box in her hands.

He took off his sunglasses. She looked just as polished as she had before, her white pants ironed perfectly, her blue blouse crisp and neat. But an air of exhaustion accompanied her.

"Hello there," he said. "I wasn't expecting to see you come around that corner."

"Uh-oh… Is that good or bad?" she asked with a smile.

"It's good, of course." And it was. Reading Carter's reports had generated a whole new set of questions. Bishop could make the most of the opportunity and ask her some of them. The fact that he kept comparing her to every other woman he saw didn't figure into the matter.

"Are you here to visit with Sarah?" she asked.

"I am. Is she here?"

"She's in the back. Waiting for you. I just dropped by to deliver a few things."

"New pieces for your show?"

"How'd you know about that?"

"I'm a detective. I figure things out."

She started to say something, but then he pointed to the flyer in the window.

She smiled wryly. "Maybe I *should* have called you last night."

"Why?"

She pursed her lips as if she wished she could take back her words but it was too late.

"Did something happen?" he pressed.

"It's silly," she said.

"Tell me anyway."

She tightened her grip on the empty box. "Someone kept ringing my doorbell. I'd hear it, go to the door and look out, but no one was there. They rang it three times."

"When did this happen?"

"After midnight."

He frowned. "You *should* have called me."

"It was probably some kids in the neighborhood. There weren't any cars parked on the street. Just someone playing a prank, I'm sure."

"Well, I'm not. If it happens again, you need to phone me. You have the card I gave you, don't you? It's got all my numbers on it."

Her expression turned uncertain. "Do you think…" She hesitated, then tried again. "You don't think it could be connected to Kenneth's death, do you?"

"What do you think?"

"That did cross my mind," she confessed. "But why? And how?"

"Those are good questions," he said. "Maybe we need to see if we can find the answers."

Before Anise could reply, Sarah Levy appeared from behind the wall that was suspended beside them. She wore rubber-soled shoes and he found himself wondering how much she'd heard.

She looked at him, then glanced pointedly at her watch. It was made of black rubber, too, but diamonds filled the dial. "You're late."

"Yes, I am," he said in a pleasant voice.

When he said nothing else, she turned to Anise, her voice becoming brighter. "And so are you! You're going to miss your hair appointment if you don't take off."

"You're right." She acknowledged Sarah then her eyes returned to Bishop's, their color leaching in the hot sunshine pouring through the gallery's windows. "Call me later?" she asked, surprising him. "I want to finish this conversation."

"I will," he said.

She walked out the door and Bishop found himself following her progress. When he turned to Sarah Levy, he realized she was doing the same thing. She watched Anise until she went around the corner, then she faced him again. "Let's go back to my office."

The interview was short and concise. In stark contrast to Donna Capanna, Sarah answered his questions completely and without hesitation. In twenty minutes, they were finished, Sarah confirming everything Robin Estes had said when he'd spoken with her earlier. After Anise had left Sarah, Robin had arrived. They'd stayed at the shop another forty-five minutes or so, then they'd seen the police cars. They'd walked down the street and realized what had happened. She had no idea who would want Kenneth dead and if that was all Bishop needed, then she had to get back to work.

She led him out of her office, clearly

anxious to get rid of him. His steps came to a halt before the wall where Anise's boxes were on display.

"I have to confess I don't understand these." Bishop gestured toward the shadow boxes.

"Anise is an extremely talented artist." Sarah removed a speck of dust from the top of one of the pieces, her pride obvious. "Her work is also very complex. Not too many people *do* get it."

"I don't know many artists." He continued to play dumb, though it wasn't much of an act in this case. "Will Capanna's death impact her work?"

"She doesn't produce widgets," Sarah answered sharply. "Of course she'll be affected by it. But not in the way you think."

"How so?"

"Anise has had a tough life," she replied. "That's one of the reasons her pieces are so complicated."

"'A tough life'? Can you be more specific?"

"That's not for me to explain," she said firmly.

"Anise doesn't look like someone I'd describe that way," he pushed.

"Her appearance is deceiving. You would think all she does is lunch with the ladies but that's only her style. Her substance goes much deeper. She internalizes everything, good and bad. Her grief will be reflected in her work. It always has been."

Bishop stilled. "Are you telling me Mr. Capanna's death will *help* her?"

"It sounds callous," she admitted, "but yes, that's what I'm saying. Kenneth was an asshole who treated Anise without the respect she deserved but Anise will be upset by his death because that's the kind of person she is." She looked out the window in the direction Anise had disappeared earlier, her expression unreadable. After a moment, she faced Bishop again. "She'll turn that grief into energy, though. It will be good for her in the long run. Pain has always been her greatest muse."

WHEN THE DOORBELL RANG that evening, Anise went still. She told herself she was acting ridiculous, then the conversation she'd had with Bishop came back. For the briefest of moments, she thought about calling him but it wasn't that late and whoever was ringing the doorbell was still ringing it. She set down the head of lettuce she'd been washing and walked to the entry, wiping her hands on the towel she had tucked into the waistband of her jeans. She wasn't going to let the doorbell buffalo her, for goodness sakes.

When she looked out the window, Brittany stood on the porch. She wore a skimpy camisole and jeans but she appeared disheveled and depressed, her expression a scowl, her makeup a mess. There was no word to describe her hair. Sympathy came over Anise in a rush. Kenneth's death was hitting her hard—the poor kid looked even more lost than she usually did. Even though Brittany and her father had had a much different relationship than Anise and her mother, Anise knew it didn't matter. Losing a parent left an open wound and every other event was salt pouring into it.

She pulled open the door. "Hey, Brittany," she said, her pity rising. "Come on in."

The girl shuffled over the threshold, walked into Anise's living room and stood silently in the center of it. Anise closed the door and followed her. "Are you okay?"

Brittany raised her gaze without answering, her pupils wide and dark.

Anise felt a tick of warning in her chest, the girl's calmness a stark contrast to her behavior at the reception. Something wasn't right and Anise wondered if Brittany had been the one who'd rung her doorbell previously. Before she could think better of it, Anise asked. "Did you come by late last night? Someone kept ringing my doorbell."

Brittany's eyes went wide, her gaze going over Anise's shoulder as if she were looking for a way out. A second later, it came back. "No," the girl said. "Why would I do that?"

"I don't know," Anise answered. "Maybe you needed to talk to me? Is something wrong?"

"Everything's wrong. I hate my life, my boyfriend just dumped me and my father's dead."

Anise's sympathy returned. "Oh, honey...
Why don't you sit down, and we'll talk?"

Brittany didn't move. Anise took her arm
and gently guided her to the couch, but
Brittany refused to sit.

"C'mon," Anise urged. "Sit down and
talk to me."

"I don't want to talk," Brittany said in a
wooden voice. "I want the truth."

"The truth about what?"

"About my dad. I want to know about
the money and don't lie to me, either."

Disquiet rippled through Anise, even
stronger now. She stood up again, her mind
absorbing the girl's words and trying to
make sense of them. "What money?"

"The money he left me," Brittany said.
"I know he had a will. He was a lawyer.
And I know I'm getting everything so
don't try and make me think something
else, okay? Where is it?"

Comprehension brought more pity and
Anise found herself trying to touch the
girl's shoulder but Brittany stiffened and
drew back.

"Brittany, sweetie… Did your mother send you over here to ask me about this?"

She clenched her jaw. "She doesn't know I'm here. This is my thing. Just tell me the truth."

Anise doubted her, but she answered regardless. "Your father didn't have a will, Brittany. I told him more than once to take care of that but he didn't do it. He'd say he was going to then he'd get busy doing something else and—"

"Then what happens to the money?"

"There is no money," Anise said softly. "Even if he'd had a will it wouldn't have mattered."

The teenager's face went blank, her shock genuine, her dismay obvious.

"He had no assets. He could hardly pay his half of the house you and your mom live in, Britt. Some months I had to do that for him."

"You're lying."

"No." Anise shook her head. "I'm telling you the truth."

"I don't believe you."

"I'm sorry," Anise said helplessly. "I really am, but it's not a lie. If your father had left you anything, I would be the first person to tell you about it. He didn't do that, though. He didn't *have* anything to leave to anyone."

"You're keeping it all for yourself," the teenager said from behind gritted teeth. "There *had* to be money. Didn't he have, like, insurance or something?"

"No. There was no insurance. There are no assets. There's nothing but bills adding up at the office."

Brittany's black-rimmed eyes blinked in shock. A moment passed, and then Kenneth's daughter turned and went to the door. Her hand on the doorknob, she stared Anise down. "You're lying," she said in a throaty growl. "You're lying to me just like Dad used to and I'm not gonna let you get away with it, either. Not now and not ever."

THE EMPEROR'S GRAND PALACE was neither grand nor a palace. Bishop had to assume there was no emperor, either. There was plenty of food, however, and the menu went on for six pages. He closed it and ordered a bowl of hot and sour soup with iced tea to drink. While the waitress was still scribbling his order, he asked for David Wui. She looked at him with sleepy eyes.

"He owns the place, doesn't he?" Bishop asked. "His name is on the tax rolls."

She nodded her head three times then shuffled off through a set of swinging doors. The Chinese man who approached Bishop's table two minutes later was older than Bishop expected. Or maybe he just looked that way. As he neared, Bishop realized the hair he'd thought was gray had been dyed a dirty blond. It looked strange above his black eyes.

He wiped his hands on the apron he wore then held up his palms in a gesture of innocence. "I only hire legals," he said, "They all got green cards. That's what they told me. If there's a problem, I don't—"

"I'm not with ICE," Bishop said. "Cool your jets."

"But you're a cop," the man said. "I can spot a cop a mile away."

"I don't give a rat's ass who you got in the kitchen. I'm with Homicide."

"Homicide? What do you want with me?"

Bishop nodded toward the other side of his booth. "Why don't you sit down and we'll talk about it."

The guy threw a nervous look over his shoulder before he seemed to realize he didn't have a choice. He sat down and removed a pack of cigarettes from his apron pocket, lighting one with nicotine-stained fingers.

Bishop reached into one of his own pockets and pulled out the photograph he'd snapped while in Donna Capanna's kitchen. Following a hunch he'd had since learning the origin of Capanna's last call and seeing the guest list from the service, he slid the picture across the table and watched the other man's face.

"Who is she?"

It was obvious Wui wanted to lie because he didn't know what the woman had done but with Bishop staring him down, the man had to tell the truth. He looked up from the photo of the Asian woman in a bright pink dress. "That's my sister, Lei," he said reluctantly. A look of alarm crossed his expression. "Is she—"

"She's fine," Bishop said, "but I need to know where I can find her."

"She lives off Richmond. I can give you her phone number but I want to know why."

Bishop ignored the man's request. Instead, he slid a second photograph over the top of the table. Robin had given it to Bishop the day he'd searched Kenneth Capanna's office. The picture had been taken several years before for an article in the *Houston Business Journal*. The "up-and-coming" tax attorney had been featured in it. "Do you know this man?"

Wui took a nervous drag on his cigarette then blew the smoke out of the side of his mouth. "That's her boyfriend," he said. "She brings him here for dinner sometimes. They been together a couple of years. They were gonna get married but…" He shrugged his shoulders, giving up his pretense.

"I took the photograph of your sister at a private memorial service for this man held on Sunday evening. You wouldn't know where your sister was Friday night, would you?"

"I don't have a clue," he said quickly.

"Really? That's strange." Bishop scratched his head and watched the waitress approach with his soup. He waited until she set down the bowl before answering Wui's second "why?" Wui knew the answer to this question as well.

"She called him right before he was killed."

"So? How would I know where she was calling from?"

"She used your telephone," Bishop said. "The one in the back. Mr. Capanna received a phone call right before he was murdered and we traced the call to this address. If it *was* your sister who contacted him, she was quite upset with him." He leaned across the table. "Why did you lie to me, Mr. Wui? You knew Kenneth Capanna had been killed and you knew your sister made the call from here. Do you think she might have had something to do with his death?"

The man on the other side of the table stamped out his cigarette and stood. Scribbling a number and an address on the back of a napkin he pulled from the dispenser, he shoved it across the table. "Ask her yourself. She's a big girl."

Wui vanished behind the swinging doors a second later. Throwing some bills on the table, Bishop left without touching the soup to head for the address written on the crumpled paper.

ANISE COULDN'T BELIEVE it when the doorbell rang an hour later. Was Brittany back already? What would Anise do if the teenager was there once more? Her questions had been heartbreaking to Anise. Brittany had never wanted for anything but she'd inherited her mother's method of measuring love. She needed a final sign from Kenneth that she meant something to him. And to her that meant money, just like it did to Donna.

Anise left her studio wondering how she was going to handle the situation. When she got to the door, however, Brittany wasn't on the porch.

Bishop was.

Relief swept over her, and a tiny flash of anticipation followed. *Bishop was here, he could handle anything*…. Shocked by her response, she pushed it away, opening the door and letting the cop inside.

"I know it's late," he said, "but I thought I'd drop by instead of calling. Would you like that update or am I interrupting anything important?"

"An update would be great." Still reeling from her reaction, she answered him quickly. "I'm glad to see you and not who I was expecting…"

She closed the door in time to see him stop midstride. They were inches apart, his attitude switching from casual to intense in a matter of seconds.

"Who were you expecting?" he demanded.

His nearness unsettled her even more. Using her words as a shield, she moved past him and pointed to the couch. "Can we sit?"

He followed her into the living room. She took the chair and he took the couch. His ever-present notebook came out but he laid it on the cushion beside him as she started to talk.

"Brittany came by about an hour ago,"

she began. "I'm pretty sure she was the one who rang my doorbell Sunday night, too." She told him of the girl's demands.

He absorbed the information. "Poor kid... Did her father lie to her often?"

"He wasn't the best dad in the world. He would promise to show up then find an excuse not to. He would forget her birthday. He could definitely have done better."

"Does Donna keep any weapons at home?"

Not really surprised by the question, Anise thought about her answer. "Donna hunts. The whole family does, her mother, her father...all of them. They must have rifles around but..." She took a second and gathered herself. "You don't think Brittany could have shot her dad, do you?"

"What do you think?"

"I don't know," she said. "I guess anything is possible. I did wonder if that was her on the phone that night."

"I've asked Donna's permission to talk to her. We'll have to wait and see. I don't want to get a court order unless I have to."

She nodded and the silence between

them grew, Anise's thoughts going back to Brittany's visit. Should she tell him she thought the girl might have been high? She couldn't decide because she wasn't sure. She thought Brittany's pupils had been dilated but she certainly wasn't a doctor. Maybe the teenager was taking a prescription of some sort, something to help her adjust to her father's death.

She argued with herself until she felt Bishop's stare. She raised her eyes to his. "What?" she asked.

"You want to tell me something more about your conversation?"

He'd sensed her dilemma. She tried not to show her surprise but she wasn't sure she succeeded. She wasn't accustomed to men who could read her mind. Kenneth had been so oblivious to anything outside himself she didn't know how to react.

"No," she said slowly. "That's all."

Their gazes connected over the coffee table. He had hazel eyes, she realized for the first time, a cross between green and gold. Their color reminded her of a tiny piece of granite she'd used once in a box, its polish so perfect she'd been able to see a minuscule reflection of herself in its surface.

"Are you sure?"

Her mouth went dry. "I'm sure."

He stared at her for another second, then seemed to accept her answer. She let out a silent breath of relief.

"Then I guess I need to tell you why I came over."

She nodded.

"I know who called Kenneth right before he was shot."

CHAPTER SEVEN

ANISE LEANED TOWARD HIM, her movement sending a hint of perfume…and paint in his direction. The combination was a pleasant one. Which made his news even harder to understand. Why would Kenneth Capanna have had a mistress if he'd had a wife like her?

"Her name is Lei Wui," he said. "The trace we put on the call Kenneth got on his cell phone that night showed that it was placed from a Chinese restaurant down on Sage. I interviewed the owner and showed him a photo of a woman who was at the memorial service on Sunday. He admitted she was his sister. She wouldn't have had time to get from the restaurant to the scene to do the shooting herself."

"The Chinese woman in the fuchsia dress," Anise said faintly.

"You noticed her?"

"It was impossible not to," she said. "The dress was so bright. And she was so beautiful," she added.

"I went to her apartment to talk to her but she wasn't there. I'll have to go back. But she definitely knew your husband. Her brother confirmed it."

Anise didn't respond. She simply stared at him in silence and waited for more.

"They'd been together for almost two years. Her brother told me she thought they were going to marry."

Anise blinked. "Two years? We were only married one year. He must have been with her even when we were dating."

"It seems that way."

"When you asked me Friday night whether or not he had a girlfriend, I thought you meant right now, not when we were actually together. Two years?" Her gaze went out the window behind the couch where he sat, then it came back. "I found something in one of his jackets once.

A napkin from a Chinese restaurant we'd never been to. It seemed like an odd thing to keep so I remembered it. There were other signs, too. I ignored them as well."

"Like what?"

"Charges on the credit card. Mysterious phone calls. That kind of thing."

"He never said anything about her?"

"No."

Bishop studied the woman in front of him. She was telling him the truth now. She'd been lying earlier. The teenager had told Anise more than she'd admitted. He'd wanted to press Anise but this wasn't the time.

Bishop forced himself back to the task at hand. "But if he'd told her they were going to marry then why didn't he want a divorce?"

"Who knows? Kenneth operated by a set of rules that he made up as he went along. He must have changed his mind."

"Obviously, but why? She said he wasn't 'getting away' with this when she called, right?"

"That's what she said," Anise replied

with a grimace. "And she was angry enough to be a woman scorned, if you know what I mean."

He felt sorry for Anise. She clearly hadn't loved the guy but still… Shaking his head, he dismissed his feelings of sympathy. He was conducting a homicide investigation, he reminded himself, and he couldn't afford to forget it.

Still, knowing better but unable to stop himself, he spoke quietly. "I'm sorry. When someone is killed like this, a lot of loose ends are left hanging. They aren't always pleasant to deal with."

"I've handled worse."

He stared at her through the lamplight, the subtle glow turning her hair a darker red, Sarah's words about a hard life coming back to him. "How is that?"

"It's not important."

"It is to me."

"When you don't have parents to rely on, you grow up fast." She shrugged. "But we all have different coping mechanisms, right? You told me already you work a lot yourself."

"I do, but the things I have to deal with aren't like this."

"What do you mean? You have to face this kind of thing all the time."

"The situations aren't personal." He looked at her. "My divorce was the worst emotional storm I ever had to weather. I have a feeling you wouldn't say that."

She kept her expression neutral. "Probably not."

He waited for more, but just like before, she didn't give it.

There was nothing else he could do. Rising from his spot on the couch, he turned and started for the entry, Anise right behind him. When they reached the door, though, she spoke instead of opening it for him.

"So what *do* you do?" she asked. "To cope, I mean?"

He wasn't sure why but he got the impression she didn't want him to leave. He wondered if she was lonely. "I do volunteer work," he said. "With the HPD Children's Charity organization. They send me to the medical center downtown. I go in once a week and talk to the kids in the cancer wing, interact with them, stuff like that. It puts a lot of things into perspective. Blanco and I have been doing it for years."

"Blanco?"

"My dog. I'm gone so much he really thinks he belongs to my dog-sitter, Brenda, the kid down the block, but when we are together we have a great time. He loves to visit the kids and they love him, too. In fact, we're having our annual fund-raiser in a couple of weeks and I'm responsible for all the auction items. It's driving me nuts."

She leaned against the wall behind her. "What are you auctioning?"

"Anything I can get my hands on," he admitted.

"Could I contribute?"

Her offer surprised him, then he wondered why. Anise had a hidden side, a softness that she protected because she thought she had to. The glimpse into her psyche made him like her even more. "That would be fantastic," he said. "What do you have in mind?"

"How about one of my boxes?" she suggested. "If I have enough time, I could make one for you."

He remembered the price tags he'd seen on her work in Sarah's studio. "Are you sure?"

"Absolutely," she said. "It would be good for me."

Their gazes met once again and Bishop thought he felt something pass between them. Anise was definitely out of his league and even more important, out-of-bounds. The captain would have a stroke if he ever found out, but what the hell? Bishop could tell him the event was nothing personal—strictly for the kids—and he might buy the story. Maybe….

"I'll take it," he said, "but only on two conditions."

She raised an eyebrow.

"You have to come to the benefit with me and present it yourself."

"I guess I can do that. What else?"

"You have to explain it to me," he said. "No excuses about jinxes or anything like that."

"I'll do my best," she promised. "But if that doesn't work out, can I make up something instead?"

"I love a good bedtime story," he answered slowly. "Feel free to do whatever you like."

ANISE WATCHED Bishop return to his car. Then she closed her front door and leaned her head against it. What had she just done? Had she just accepted a date?

She shook her head in denial. Of course she hadn't. She was merely making a donation for a worthy cause. It'd be good PR and bring more sales her way.

Sarah would not be happy when she learned about the generous gift but the gesture itself meant nothing more.

Straightening her shoulders, Anise decided it *couldn't* mean more. She'd meant what she'd told Sarah about never falling in love again and she meant it even more now. Bishop obviously cared about the kids he was helping, though, and his attitude had made her want to do something as well. Heading back to the kitchen, she wondered why he had picked that particular cause. She made a mental note to ask him. He didn't strike her as a man who made random choices.

Unlike Kenneth.

Anise walked around the end of the kitchen island but instead of tackling her dinner dishes, she sat down on the bar stool, her mind returning to the news Bishop had delivered.

Kenneth had had a mistress the entire time they'd been married.

The idea stung more than she cared to admit even though theirs hadn't been the greatest love of all time. What had he needed that she'd been unable to provide? A list of things came immediately to her mind—more attention, more sex, more… everything. What did it matter now, though? Their marriage had been dead long before Kenneth was.

She sat for another ten minutes, contemplating Kenneth and his mistress, but no answers came. Finally she rose from the stool, finished the dishes, then got the trash ready to take out. She hadn't slept much in days. She hoped tonight her lack of rest would catch up with her. As soon as she was done in the kitchen, she'd take a hot bath then fall into bed.

Opening the back door, she stepped out into the night. The air was still and warm, and down the street someone's television blared. Turning away from the curb where she'd dropped the plastic bag, she started back for the house.

She was halfway there when a shadow detached itself from the darkness and rushed toward her.

STEERING WITH ONE HAND and reaching for his phone with the other, Bishop merged onto I10. It was late but traffic was still heavy. Muscling the Crown Vic between a eighteen-wheeler hauling pipe and a speeding jackass in a pickup, he started down the freeway. He would try Lei Wui once more before heading home. He wanted to talk to Kenneth's mistress as soon as possible.

He patted the seat beside him with the hand that held the phone but his notebook was nowhere to be found. A second later, he cursed. He'd left it on Anise's couch.

There was nothing he could do but turn around and go back. He'd call her first though. Not surprisingly, *her* number was one he had in his head. He tried not to analyze that fact too closely.

He punched out her number and let it ring six times.

When she didn't answer, he frowned. He'd left her house only minutes ago. Where could she have gone in such a short time? She hadn't indicated to him she was leaving. He hit the redial button, but something told him she wasn't going to answer. He thought about her conversation with Brittany Capanna and his mind took him in a direction he didn't want to go.

Ignoring a chorus of horns and outstretched middle fingers, he cut across three lanes of traffic and exited the freeway. Five minutes later he pulled onto her street.

ANISE STUMBLED backward with a cry, catching herself at the last minute. The shadow kept coming, then stopped in a patch of brightness from the streetlight overhead.

Relief followed by anger swept over Anise. "For God's sake, Robin! You scared me half to death! What are you doing out here? Why didn't you come to the front door?"

"I saw you taking out the trash," the other woman said. "I came this way instead. It seemed easier."

Her voice was strained and edgy, and the air around her seemed to vibrate with tension.

"You sound…upset," Anise said. "Is something wrong?"

"Nothing's wrong! There's nothing wrong with me. Nothing!"

Anise stopped in the center of the driveway. First Brittany and now this. She'd had enough drama for one night. "What do you want, Robin? I'm tired. I'm on my way to bed. Is there something you needed?"

The secretary unexpectedly burst into tears, her shoulders shaking as she sobbed. "I love her," she cried. "All I've ever wanted was to love her and have her love me back and she won't do it!" Her cry turned into a hiccuped moan. "—e's gone now and she still won't do it!"

Robin sounded so heartbroken, Anise

started forward to comfort her. Had she and Sarah broken up again? "Oh, Robin, I'm sorry…"

Robin lifted her head and then her arm. She held something in her hand but it couldn't possibly be what Anise thought it was. Anise took another step but jerked to a stop when she realized she wasn't mistaken. "What?"

"Stop right there!" Robin cried. "I mean it, Anise! Stop now!"

Anise went still, the pistol in Robin's wavering grasp so incongruent she didn't know how to react. "Wh-what are you doing with a gun, Robin? For God's sake, you're going to hurt someone! Put that down!"

"It's your fault," Robin said. The weapon shook in her hands. "None of this would have ever happened if you weren't around!"

Anise stared at Robin in confusion. "What are you talking about?"

"Don't act like you don't understand."

"But I don't—"

Before she could finish, a set of headlights illuminated the driveway.

"DROP THE WEAPON and put your hands above your head!"

Kneeling into a shooter's stance, Bishop called out again.

"Put the gun down! Now!"

Robin Estes hesitated then fled, her shadow disappearing into the darkness that surrounded Anise's house.

"Call 911," he yelled as he ran by Anise, "and stay inside!"

He headed in the direction he thought the other woman had gone but thirty minutes later, she was still nowhere to be found. The uniforms who'd arrived following Anise's call continued to circle the neighborhood, and Bishop made it clear they were to keep doing so until he told them to stand down.

He found himself back in Anise's living room once more. "Tell me again what she said."

Anise repeated the secretary's accusations, shaking her head in confusion when she finished. "I have no idea what she was talking about or what she even meant. She was acting crazy!"

"I don't suppose you can tell me what kind of weapon she had?"

A furrow etched its way across Anise's forehead and Bishop found himself wondering what would have happened if he hadn't come back when he did. He decided he didn't want to think about that possibility.

"It was a big black pistol," she answered. "I don't know anything about guns but it scared me, that's for sure."

"Have you ever seen it before?"

"No! I didn't know Robin even owned one."

"Repeat her words again."

"It was something like 'she's gone now and she still won't do it.' I didn't understand at all."

"Are you sure she didn't say *'he's'* gone?"

Anise went still except for her fingers. They knit themselves together in her lap. "I…I don't think that's what she said but I was focusing more on the gun than I was on her. What are you suggesting?"

"I'm not suggesting anything," Bishop replied. "I'm just wondering. She worked for your husband. Someone shot him. She shows up with a gun. Obviously something links the two episodes."

"Robin couldn't have shot Kenneth," Anise said. "She was with Sarah, remember? But regardless, Robin wouldn't do something like that. She's too…timid, even if she had a reason, which she doesn't."

Thinking about her argument, Bishop stared at Anise as his phone rang. The cop who answered his distracted hello was the one Bishop had sent to Estes's apartment.

"No sign of her here," the woman announced. "You want me to stay put or what?"

"Don't leave," Bishop ordered. "I'll get back to you."

He hung up and explained. "I'll keep someone at Robin's apartment for a while. She might turn up." He stood up and walked to the window to look outside. With his back to Anise, he spoke. "What in the hell was she doing here? And why now? Why you?"

Anise understood that he didn't expect an answer but she stood up, too, and went to his side.

"Robin wasn't really going to shoot me."

She looked up at him, her eyes luminescent. "You aren't going to arrest her, are you?"

"She threatened you," he said with exasperation. "She had a gun. I would think you'd want her off the street."

"Robin is not capable of taking anyone's life."

"You don't know that for sure."

"Maybe not, but I do know this. She isn't stupid."

"And that changes the situation because…?"

"She lives for one thing," Anise said. "And if she shot me, her chances of winning that one thing would go out the window."

He raised an eyebrow. "And that one thing is?"

"Robin worships the ground Sarah walks on. Even if she was capable of harming me, which she isn't, her relationship with Sarah would be over if she hurt me. She'd never risk it. Not in a million years."

ANISE'S REVELATION DIDN'T surprise Bishop. She could tell by the look on his face that he'd already figured out part of the women's tangled relationship.

"They're lovers?"

"Sometimes," Anise answered. "Right now, I'm not sure where they stand. They break up and make up on a continual basis. I can't keep track."

"What's the attraction?" he asked. "Ms. Estes doesn't seem like the type Sarah Levy would be interested in. Estes seems too ordinary for someone as high energy as Sarah."

"I'm not the best person to ask that question," Anise said. "My own attempts at a lasting relationship haven't exactly been stellar."

"Maybe," Bishop conceded. "But you know them both. You could shed some light on it."

Anise liked the fact that he didn't contradict the assessment she'd made of her past love life.

Or did she?

She told herself to focus and tried to answer his question. "Robin needs someone to tell her what to do and Sarah likes to boss people around. Maybe that's the thing that keeps them together, I don't know."

He pursed his lips. "I guess I've heard of stranger connections. God only knows what kept my ex and me together."

Anise's curiosity bubbled to the surface and the question popped out before she could stop it. "How long were you married?"

"Seven years." He stopped then added, "Seven *long* years."

"No kids?"

He shook his head and a sense of regret, his first, came to her with the movement. "She said she didn't want children if she had to raise them by herself."

Anise nodded. "She was worried about your job. I can see that. It seems dangerous to me, too."

"My job didn't have anything to do with it," he said, his voice brusque. "I was never at home. That's what she meant."

Some of his earlier comments made sense now. "So life gets in the way, huh? Now you're divorced and you visit kids in the hospital."

He looked down at her, his gaze holding hers. "For someone who doesn't have a very good track record with relationships, you're pretty astute in the psychology department."

"It's the artist's eye," she replied. "We can see the truth that strangers hide but we never understand ourselves. It's a blessing and a curse."

"I'll keep that in mind," he answered. Turning to her left, he reached behind her to pick up something off the couch, his arm brushing hers in an accidental way. The touch was brief but it registered. When he straightened, he held a notebook. "The reason I came back," he explained.

She nodded, her breath suddenly tight. "Thank goodness you're forgetful."

He smiled. "We aim to please."

They stood silently in the dimly lit living room until he broke the moment by starting for the door once again. She followed, trying to hide the wave of confusion that was washing over her.

His hand on the doorknob, he spoke. "I'm keeping two men outside just in case. They'll be in their patrol car if you need them. In the meantime, stay close to home until we locate Ms. Estes."

He turned to go out the door but at the last minute, she reached out and stopped him. Beneath her fingers, his arm felt rock-solid. "Bishop?"

He looked down at her and waited.

"Thank you for what you did tonight. I really appreciate it."

"I'm glad my forgetfulness finally paid off. Usually it's just damn inconvenient."

She dropped her hand with an awkwardness she hoped he didn't notice. "I guess sometimes the traits we don't like very much are necessary, regardless. That must be why we have them."

"Maybe so," he agreed.

For a single wild second, the thought that he might lean over and kiss her crossed her mind. He left instead.

In a déjà vu moment, she shut the door behind him and closed her eyes.

CHAPTER EIGHT

WHEN ANISE WOKE the following morning she couldn't believe how heavily she'd slept. She felt as if someone had slipped her something. She was dressed and out the door by nine, though, the gallery her first and only stop. After Bishop had left, she'd tried to call Sarah too many times to count but to no avail.

Sarah smiled as Anise walked into the office but her expression faded quickly. "What's wrong?"

"Have you talked to Robin?"

"No." Sarah shook her head in obvious mystification. "Why?"

"Where were you last night?"

"I was down the street at Jilly Sloan's gallery until way after midnight. She had an opening and I walked down there after

I closed up here. What's going on? Why all the questions?"

"I tried to call you—"

"I couldn't take my phone. Jilly insists on sil—"

Anise interrupted abruptly. "Robin came by the house and scared me half to death."

"What? Are you serious? Robin couldn't scare a squirrel—"

"She had a gun," Anise said grimly. "And she was acting bizarre."

Her mouth falling open, Sarah stared at Anise in shock. "A gun? What did she want?"

Anise relayed the conversation she and Robin had shared in her driveway. "Was she talking about you, Sarah? Did you guys break up again?"

Sara came from behind her desk, her movements slow and deliberate. "We can't break up again because we aren't together in the first place."

"But you've been seeing her?"

"As a friend. Nothing more."

"That's your interpretation of the situation," Anise said. "What's Robin's?"

"The same," Sarah insisted. "I made myself very clear when she approached me this last time. We're fine as friends but I can't get involved with her again. I told her so."

Sarah never discussed her love life with Anise so in return she'd made it a policy to keep her nose out of Sarah's business. But this time she made an exception.

"And why is that?"

"It wasn't going to work out." Sarah rested a hip against the edge of her desk. "There was no sense in pursuing it. In fact, that's why we were together the night Kenneth was shot. We sat down and talked things over and agreed we'd just be friends." She started to say something more then stopped. "What happened after she spewed all this stuff?"

"She ran off," Anise said. "Bishop drove up and I guess it scared her. They looked for her, but she was long gone. And she didn't go home, either. He had an officer wait at her apartment for more than an hour, then he had to let her go. I tried to call you several times after he left but obviously that didn't work out."

"So the big, bad cop rode to your rescue?"

Anise played it cool. "He'd left something at the house when he'd dropped by earlier. He'd come back to get it."

Sarah had always had a sharp tongue, but there was even more edge to her voice when she spoke. "What did he leave? His good sense?"

"What is it with you and him?" Anise asked. "You haven't liked him from the beginning."

"I don't like his attitude," Sarah replied. "And I don't like him. He's arrogant and pushy and besides that, I don't think he knows what he's doing."

"He's *doing* his best."

"And his best isn't good enough. He should have caught Kenneth's killer by now. The longer it takes, the greater the chances are the guy's gonna get away with this."

"So now you're a crime expert?"

Sarah's expression tightened as she crossed her arms. "I think the real question is what's going on between *you* and *him?* You like him, don't you?"

"He's a nice guy and he does charity

work for children. In fact," Anise took a deep breath, "I'm making a box for him to auction off in a few weeks at the HPD Children's Charity gala. They're having a fund-raiser and I wanted to help." She kept her promise to go with Bishop to herself.

Silence built as Sarah stared at Anise. Then she smiled unexpectedly, doing a fast one-eighty.

"You know what? That's a great idea! I wish I'd thought of it myself. I'd heard about that auction but in all the confusion, I forgot about it."

Anise exhaled. "You aren't angry?"

"Angry? Why would I be upset over something like that?"

Anise ticked the reasons off using her fingers. "You don't like him. You won't make any money. I've done it before and you got mad. I'll be wasting time on it when I could be doing something else—"

Sarah stood and came to where Anise waited. Putting her hands on Anise's shoulders, she shook her head. "Listen, I'm your agent, not your mother. If you want to do this, I think you should. I'm sorry I got ticked. Your news about Robin threw me off, I guess." She squeezed Anise's arms, then released her. "It worries me, you know. We had that discussion but she hasn't been herself lately and I let it get to me."

With a feeling of relief, Anise patted Sarah in return. "It's okay," she said. "Everyone's been off-kilter since Kenneth was shot. It's hard not to be a little crazy after something like that happens. If you see Robin, though, you need to call Bishop. Or me," she added hastily. "I don't want to press charges but we need to find out what's going on with her."

"Absolutely." Sarah nodded her agreement. Then they started for the front door, their arms wrapped around each other's waists.

Pausing by the entrance, Anise put her hand on the door handle. "Thanks for understanding," she said.

"Thanks yourself," Sarah replied. "And I'll keep an eye out for Robin. Stay in touch, okay?"

"Don't worry. I'll call later."

As the door to the gallery closed behind

Anise, her cell phone began to ring. Digging through her purse, she caught it just before it rolled over to voice mail. "Hello?"

Bishop answered her greeting with a question. "Where are you?"

"Walking out of Sarah's place," she said. "What's up?"

"I just spoke with Robin Estes's neighbor," he said. "My office is a block away. Can you come by? It won't take long. I've got a meeting in ten minutes I have to go to."

He sounded serious and her pulse fluttered. "Tell me how to get there."

He gave her directions. "I'll be waiting in the lobby."

BISHOP SPOTTED Anise the second she came through the double doors of the building. She looked completely out of place, her quiet and elegant demeanor something he didn't see too often at head-quarters. Or anywhere else, he amended. She was a special person but he reminded himself quickly of how they had come together. Anything more than just a casual relationship between the two of them was something that couldn't happen. Not if he wanted to keep his job.

He called her name and she smiled as she saw him. In spite of his earlier thought, his estimation of her went higher. No one smiled very often here, either.

They met in the middle of the lobby and Bishop directed her toward the elevator, his hand on the middle of her back. "This way," he said. "I'm on the tenth floor."

They rode in silence with seven unhappy strangers. When they got off, Anise's relief was palpable. "This isn't a very cheery place, is it?"

"A lot of misery around here," he agreed. "But we occasionally do some good." As if to back him up, someone laughed down the hall.

She smiled again and he felt himself respond.

"This way," he said to cover it up. "My office is back here."

She followed him to his desk and took the chair beside it. Her question came out before he could sit. "Did you find Robin?"

"I went by her place early and rang the doorbell but no one answered. I was heading back to my car when an older woman came out of the apartment next door and stopped me. She asked if I was looking for Robin and I said yes. That's when she informed me I wasn't going to find her, at least not anytime soon."

Anise leaned forward. "Why did she say that?"

"Robin told her yesterday that she was taking an extended vacation. Said she left late that morning with two big bags to go to the airport."

Anise's expression combined both shock and confusion. "Did she say where she was going?"

"She didn't," he answered. "Does she have a place she could go, relatives that might take her in?"

"Not that I'm aware of. She was an only child. Her parents are divorced. One lives in Denver and the other one's in…Grand Forks? I'm not sure."

He jotted a note on the desk pad that covered his desk. It was already covered with scratches he could hardly read. "What about friends? Someone she might stay with for a while?"

"None that I knew about. If she and Sarah were getting along, she would hang around with us on occasion but there wasn't a real closeness. She worked for Kenneth and that was about it." Anise leaned back in the chair, a look of uncertainty coming over her delicate features. "This is so weird."

"What did Ms. Levy have to say about what happened? I tried to call her last night but she never answered. She hadn't heard from Robin, had she?"

"No. I tried to call her last night, too. She told me she was at a function where cell phones were not allowed. All she said was that Robin hadn't been herself lately but she didn't say why. She said they weren't dating anymore but had agreed to a friendship."

"Well, I'm filing the complaint this afternoon. As far as our records show, she doesn't have a permit for that handgun. I'm going to bring her in on the charge and ask her some questions."

"Is that necessary?"

"The woman went after you with a weapon. I should have filed the paperwork yesterday but I didn't have time. I think you need to realize the seriousness of this issue."

"You think that way because you're a cop."

"I think that because I care." He leaned over his desk and met her eyes. "I still don't know who shot Kenneth. In fact, I don't have a clue. But if we press charges against Robin, I can confiscate the weapon she was waving around last night. We could get a ballistics report on it. Do you understand what I'm saying?"

The color left her face. "There would be no reason for Robin to kill Kenneth."

"That's what you said about Brittany. And Donna. But he's dead. And someone pulled that trigger. It's my job to find out who."

"I'll think about it."

"Well, don't think for too long." He stood. "Time's running out and I'm not happy with the way this is going."

Back in the lobby, he held the door open

for her and they both stepped out into the bright sunshine.

"What did Ms. Levy have to say about your generous donation to my cause?"

Fumbling with the sunglasses she'd pulled from her purse, Anise looked up at him in surprise.

He shrugged. "You were there. I just assumed you two discussed it. She's your business manager, isn't she?"

Anise slipped on her glasses. "She was fine with it. As a matter of fact, she said she wished she'd thought of the idea herself."

"That's good." He didn't believe her for a minute but he decided to push his luck anyway. There came a time in every man's life where he had to take the plunge, to hell with his job. Who needed a career anyway? "Why don't we have dinner tonight and discuss what you're going to do? Or we could discuss the case? Or we could discuss whatever you like…."

He couldn't read her eyes because of the sunglasses, but he didn't need to. Her stillness answered him.

"I have to work," she said.

He tried a second time. "You have to eat, too."

"That's true. I've got a lot going though, and my show is coming up. If I don't get those pieces finished, no one else is going to do it for me. You know how that goes, don't you?"

Her excuse was a slap. How many times had he said something just like that to his ex-wife when he'd wanted to do anything but spend the evening with her? The gods must be laughing. The irony was too much.

"I understand," he said reluctantly. "We'll put the idea on hold, but Anise…"

She looked up at him.

"Keep your doors locked and keep the phone handy. Until I track down Estes and clear this up, you need to be careful. She's obviously unhappy with you for some reason."

WHAT WAS SHE DOING? What was she doing? What was she doing?

Climbing into her ovenlike car, Anise started the engine and drove home on automatic pilot. By the time she reached her street she'd managed to convince herself she'd done the right thing.

She wasn't interested in starting a new relationship.

She wanted to concentrate on her work.

Daniel Bishop was not her type.

The arguments rang false but she was determined to stick to her decision. The weekend came and she left her studio only once, to get groceries. Sarah called her twice and they talked about Robin but nothing came of the discussion. Sarah had no idea Robin had been planning a vacation and knew nothing about it. Putting the incident behind her, Anise immersed herself in the details of the few remaining boxes she had to finish for the show before turning her attention to the one she wanted to build for Bishop's auction.

The perfect idea came to her late on Sunday but it was so out of character she immediately dismissed it. The harder she tried to focus on something else, though, the more insistent the design became. Finally she picked up her pencil and began to sketch.

She was so involved she didn't hear the

phone ring at first, then finally the insistent noise registered. She answered with distraction, her head tilted slightly as she stared at her sketch, one pencil in her mouth, one stuck behind her ear.

"Anise?"

Bishop's puzzled voice registered instantly and she yanked the pencil from between her teeth. "Yes," she said. "It's me…"

"Is everything okay?"

"I'm fine," she said. "I was working. I had a pencil in my mouth and—"

His manner was curt as he interrupted her explanation. "Why didn't you tell me Kenneth had an apartment?"

"An apartment?" She sat down on the stool behind her, shock rippling over her. "I didn't know he had one," she answered. "I thought he'd been staying at his office. There's a kitchen and bath there… Nothing big but… He has—had—an apartment? How did you figure that out?"

"How doesn't matter," he said. "I need to get in and look around. Tonight. Can you bring some ID and meet me there?

The manager wants a warrant or a family member."

"Give me the address."

"It's at 12010 Richmond. They're called the Holly Springs Apartments."

"I'll be there in twenty minutes."

"I'm downtown. It may take me longer. Wait for me."

"No problem. I'll see you there."

She hung up the phone and sat frozen in surprise. Good grief. What kind of secret life had Kenneth led? A mistress? An apartment? What else had he been hiding? How could she have been so oblivious to everything? Not wanting to examine that idea too closely, she grabbed the piece of paper with the address and strode down the hall to her bedroom. Jerking a jacket from the closet, she picked up her purse and went out to the garage, her head spinning once more.

The complex held less than sixty units and was brand new, judging by the fresh paint and luxurious landscaping. A note on the door of the office listed a telephone number along with a woman's name,

Yolanda Bentley, and the word *Manager* spelled out beneath it. Bentley answered on the third ring and told Anise she'd meet her at the apartment. "It's 15B," she explained. "Faces the back. In the corner. It's one of our nicer units."

A few moments later, Anise parked in front of the apartment where a tall black woman waited for her, a set of keys dangling in her hand. She greeted Anise as she stepped from the car, then looked at the identification Anise offered.

"I'm so sorry to hear about your husband," the woman said, her dark eyes filled with genuine sympathy. "But how do I know you're really his wife? That driver's license says you're Anise Borden."

"Oh, dear, you're right. I kept my maiden name when we married." Anise reached back inside her bag for her wallet. She thumbed through the plastic insert that contained photographs she had yet to remove. One had been shot at their wedding, Anise in a long white dress, Kenneth in his tux. She held it out to the woman. "Would this work? It was taken when we got married."

The woman glanced at it with an embarrassed expression. "That's fine," she said, "and I'm sorry I even have to ask, but you know how it is. If the boss found out, I had let someone else in…"

"It's okay," Anise answered. "I understand."

"Thank you," the manager said. "I thought you would. When your husband rented the apartment, he was so worried about whether or not you would like it. I got the impression you were someone special."

Stuffing her wallet back into her purse, Anise didn't know what to say. "Is…is that right?"

"Oh, yes. He said he selected a place you would like since you weren't crazy about moving here from New York to begin with." She patted Anise's arm as they made their way to the door, speaking over her shoulder. "I was shocked when the policeman called and told me what happened."

"So was I," Anise said.

The woman unlocked the door then reached inside and flipped on a light. "I'm gonna go on back to my place," she said.

"Y'all just take your time. When you finish up, lock the door on your way out. We can settle up later."

She started down the sidewalk but Anise stopped her. "Ms. Bentley? Did Kenneth owe you any rent? I…I can't quite remember exactly when he signed the lease."

"We're fine," the apartment manager said. "I looked up the paperwork after the policeman called me. Mr. Capanna paid for six months up front. I told him he didn't have to do it that way but he insisted. And that was only last month so you got five more."

Anise thanked the woman, then stepped inside and closed the door behind her. Kenneth had been protesting the divorce but he'd had a rented apartment ready to go. What kind of sense did that make?

The rental smelled like stale furniture polish and an air of depression hung over it. She dropped her purse on the floor beside the door and surveyed the interior. The barest of necessities had been placed in the center of the front room. A couch, a table, two chairs. A lonely glass sat beside the sink in the kitchen but that was it.

Walking down the hall, she paused. The room on the right held a bed and nothing more. The room on the left had a desk with a laptop computer on it.

She stood quietly and listened. Nothing broke the silence. Not even traffic noise. Why had Kenneth kept this place a secret? She wouldn't have been surprised to find he'd finally rented a place. In fact, she would have welcomed it as a sign he was moving on.

She explored the apartment, ending up in the bathroom. It was as empty as the kitchen, except for a single bottle of perfume sitting on the countertop. She picked it up and sniffed at the top. The scent was spicy and strong. Closing her eyes, she imagined the Chinese woman dabbing it on her perfect skin. The fragrance was something she could have worn. It would have overpowered Anise.

Setting the bottle back where she found it, Anise went into the closet next. It was as empty as the rest of the place.

Her puzzlement growing, she stepped into the office and sat behind at the desk. The laptop resembled one Kenneth had had but she wasn't sure it was his. They all looked the same to her. She hesitated, then she gave in to her curiosity and tapped the touch pad. The monitor came to life with a standard Microsoft screen asking for a password.

She stared at the blinking cursor and told herself to leave it alone but she couldn't. Moving the pointer to the login window, she held her fingers over the keyboard for a second before entering the date of Kenneth's birth. The machine's drive whirred, the sound loud in the silence of the apartment. Outlook—and all Kenneth's e-mails—appeared on the display.

He had them organized by date and the last one he'd received had been from Robin.

Anise clicked on the e-mail and scanned the note, the words making as much sense as the gun Robin had held during her unexpected appearance the week before. Hearing a small sound she looked up to find Bishop in the doorway.

"I told you to wait for me."

CHAPTER NINE

ANISE'S GAZE MET Bishop's over the top of the monitor. He'd stopped himself half a dozen times from calling her in the past few days. When he'd found out about the apartment, he'd pumped his fist and whispered "yes." The place might give him the break he needed in the case, but it also provided him a good reason to get in touch with her as well. As long as he could claim it was necessary for the investigation…

"I didn't think you meant to wait outside."

He could tell she was being honest. The idea had never entered her mind that it might be dangerous for her to go into the apartment without him. Bishop didn't know if that was a good thing or not.

"Did you touch anything besides the computer?"

She blushed. "There's a bottle of perfume in the bathroom. I picked it up."

"It's not yours, I take it?"

She shook her head. "I had no idea Kenneth had this apartment, Bishop. When you called and told me, I was shocked. Ask the manager. She'll tell you she never saw me before tonight. How did you find it?"

He walked into the bedroom and came to the desk. "I emptied his desk last week. I had Carter look at everything but he said he didn't find anything. When I decided to look for myself, I found a receipt for the rent."

"I guess it's a good thing you did." She nodded and motioned him closer. "Look at this."

He moved to her side and leaned over, his hands spread on either side of the laptop. He could smell her shampoo.

Then he read the e-mail. Robin Estes's name was in the sender box.

I did everything you wanted me to do, Kenneth, but you aren't holding up your end of the bargain. I don't know what else to do but I think we need to reconsider our plans. I'm not happy with the way things are going and I think we'd both agree that I need to be happy.

Bishop looked at Anise. Her face was inches from his and the impression he'd had of her that first night came back to him full force. She looked ethereal.

To distract himself, he tilted his head toward the screen. "What do you think she's talking about?"

"I don't know." She pulled her bottom lip in between her teeth then let it go. "Obviously they were doing something together but Kenneth wasn't living up to his part of it. Surprise, surprise…."

Bishop read the note again. "Could it have something to do with work?"

"I doubt it," Anise said.

He did, too. "Are there other e-mails?"

"Yes. I looked at that one because it was the last note he received but there are more."

"From Robin?"

She nodded. "And from other people, too. I think I saw some from Brittany."

He straightened. "I'll need to take the

machine in and let the tech guys investigate. They can get everything off it. If I start messing with it, I could screw it up."

She stood up and pushed the chair back. "What do you think this means?"

"I think it means I better find Robin Estes."

BISHOP INSISTED on driving her home. "I'll have one of the guys bring your car back later," he said. "We'll have plenty of folks there going over the apartment. When one of them finishes, they can deliver it."

"But why—"

"I don't want you going home alone." He answered her question before she could finish. "I want to check your doors and windows, too. Just to be safe. Do you have an alarm system?"

"No."

"You might want to think about getting one." He looked over at her. "Or a guard dog."

His intensity frightened her. She tried to lighten the moment. "Is Blanco busy? Maybe I could borrow him?"

Bishop made a sound that was a cross

between a laugh and disgust. "Blanco? He might lick a burglar to death but other than that, you wouldn't want to count on him for protection." His mood turned somber. "And I think you need some. Robin Estes is not a stable person."

Anise looked out the window, shook her head, then stared at him, her earlier confusion returning full force. "What was Kenneth doing? Why would he have rented an apartment and not tell me?"

"You *were* divorcing. It would make sense. He wouldn't want to stay at his office forever."

"It didn't look as if he were planning to live there. It was basically empty."

"Except for the perfume."

She nodded. Then looked out the window again.

"I talked to her Friday," he said in the silence. "She said she's been out of town but would come by my office. We made an appointment."

Anise didn't need to ask him who he meant—she knew it was Lei Wui. "What will you ask her?"

"The same questions I've asked everyone else."

The rest of the drive went by in a blur. When they reached her house, Bishop took her keys. "Let me go inside first," he said. "You wait here."

She wanted to argue, but overwhelmed by everything that had happened, she nodded instead. Opening her front door, he disappeared from sight for about five minutes before he came back to the front porch and motioned for her.

"This feels silly," she said when she reached his side. "You don't really think I'm in any kind of danger, do you? Whoever killed Kenneth could have shot me at the same time if they'd wanted me dead, and Robin had her opportunity the other night."

"Maybe," he said, "Maybe not. Who knows? Either way, if it's all the same to you, I'd just as soon not give anyone another chance."

He followed her into the house and Anise looked up at him. They were close, so close that Anise knew if she had a brain in her head, she would step back and give herself some room. But she didn't.

She stood still as he raised his hand to tuck a strand of hair behind her ear. For a heartbeat, his fingers rested on her jaw and he started to lean forward.

But he stopped himself.

Anise let out the breath she was holding as Bishop moved away from her. She wasn't completely sure what she would have done had he continued. Pushing aside her reaction, she moved to the table in the entry as casually as she could, dropping her purse on its glass top. She slipped out of her jacket and turned back to face him.

They stared at each other but the moment was gone. Anise told herself she was glad.

"Will you call me after your guys examine the computer?" She spoke as if nothing had happened. "I'd like to know what you find out."

"As soon as we get something, I'll call."

"Thank you for bringing me home and looking around, Bishop. I appreciate it."

"You're welcome," he said. His eyes warmed and she felt her pulse flutter. "But

I meant what I said about a burglar alarm system. It wouldn't hurt regardless. This *is* Houston, after all."

Anise locked the door behind him when he left, the feeling of safety and security that she'd always enjoyed inside her home going with him. Her thoughts still swirling, she returned to her studio and the work that sustained her.

BY THE TIME Bishop got back to the apartment, the computer geeks had come and gone. They'd taken Capanna's machine and left a message in its stead: Don't call us, we'll call you.

The rest of the apartment offered no clues. The techs bagged the perfume bottle and the glass by the sink, dusted the furniture for prints then packed up and left as well.

Bishop wandered through the empty rooms and cursed. Anise was depending on him. And he had nothing to give her. His irritation arose from the fact they'd found so little in the apartment but it had just as much to do with the interrupted moment at her house. He'd really wanted to kiss her and for some reason, he thought she'd felt the same way. But some vestige of good sense had stopped him. Dating someone related to a case was never a good idea. He preached the fact to the rookies he sometimes trained, for God's sakes. What kind of fool was he turning into? He left the apartment in a very bad mood.

But on Monday morning, his attitude changed.

And by Monday afternoon, the whole case changed.

Lei Wui came into Bishop's office at 11:00 a.m. Their appointment had been for 9:00 a.m. Most of the cops who watched her sway down the hall wouldn't have cared that she was two hours late but Bishop was fuming by the time she entered his office. Every minute counted as far as he was concerned. He didn't think she was all that much, anyway. Just as he had with Donna Capanna, he found himself comparing her to Anise, and just like Donna, Lei Wui fell way short. There *was* no comparison to be made between her and Anise.

He had to acknowledge, however, that

the Asian woman was beautiful. Dark, shining hair, mysterious eyes, a body that was lithe yet seductive. She had all the right parts but the whole wasn't…enough.

Behind the makeup and hair and polished appearance, her attitude was surly, her manner offensive.

"I don't know why you made me come here," she said, taking the chair beside his desk. "My brother told you everything there is to know."

"I need to hear it from you," Bishop said politely. "I'm sure there are details about your relationship with Mr. Capanna that your brother didn't know."

"Kenny told me we were going to get married," she answered, her voice sharp. "But he lied. Nothing else matters."

"You'd been seeing him a long time?"

"Two years," she said.

"And did you know he was married during that time?"

"Yes."

Bishop waited but she gave him nothing more.

"That didn't bother you?"

"He loved me. He was getting a divorce. We were going to marry."

"Tell me about the night he died. You called him and you weren't too happy with him then."

Her dark eyes widened. "How—"

"He didn't answer the phone," Bishop said. "Someone else did. They relayed the message to us."

Her jaw went tight. "I was upset. I didn't mean what I said."

"You threatened to kill him."

"I *threatened*, yes. That's all."

"Why were you so upset?"

She hesitated for the first time. Looking down at the strap of her purse, she wrapped it around her wrist then unwrapped it. Finally she spoke. "Kenny said as soon as the divorce was final that we would marry. But it was taking too long. I didn't like that."

"Did he explain the delay?"

"No."

"But you were angry about it?"

"Of course!"

"Angry enough to have him killed?"

She looked at him with open scorn.

"Why would I do something like that, Mr. Bishop? I don't need to kill men. Lovers are plentiful."

The logic escaped him, but he believed her.

"You can ask my grandmother if you want to know where I was," she offered. "After I left my brother's restaurant, I went to her nursing home. It's off Bellaire. The nurses can confirm my presence. I went there because I was so upset. She calmed me down. I wouldn't have had enough time to go downtown then to her place. You can check."

He had. The Wui family, he'd learned after meeting her brother, was well-known in Chinatown and well-respected, too. He switched gears, returning to the real reason he'd wanted to talk to her—to see if he could gain more information. "Do you have any idea who might have wanted Mr. Capanna dead?"

She shook her head. "None whatsoever."

He remembered the perfume in the apartment. "Were you going to move in with Mr. Capanna any time soon?"

"We'd been looking at houses," she said.

"What about the apartment on Richmond? That wasn't going to be your home?"

She looked at him with disgust. "That dump? Are you kidding? He just used it for work."

"For work? What kind of work?"

"I don't know. Same thing he did at his office, I guess. We were looking at houses off Memorial."

Bishop leaned back in his chair. "Memorial? That's a pretty pricey area, isn't it?"

"Kenny was a lawyer," she said, smoothing her hair back. "He had plenty of money."

Bishop was still absorbing her words when one of the lab techs stuck his head through the office doorway. "We got your computer cleaned. It's ready to roll."

"Thanks. I'll be there in five."

Bishop returned to the woman, handing her one of his cards that he pulled from his desk drawer. "If you remember anything helpful, you can call me at that number," he said.

She accepted the card without a word

then left. A moment later she was around the corner and out of sight but her puzzling words remained on his mind.

Anise had told Bishop Capanna never had enough money. Now his mistress said he had plenty.

Someone was lying.

THE HAMMER HIT with just the right amount of force. The marble shattered but the pieces were large enough to use. Picking through them with a pair of tweezers, Anise singled one out, its blue and green streaks glistening in the afternoon sun. Swinging back to the box at her elbow, she dropped the fragment into the cotton she'd already glued to the back of the box. The colorful chunk fell into the perfect spot, the angles exactly how she wanted them. Grabbing the digital camera she kept handy, she pushed her magnifying glasses into her hair then clicked off two shots. She dropped the camera on the work bench and glanced at the clock behind her.

She'd been working for four hours. It was time to take a break, despite the fact that the box needed to be finished at the end of the week to be ready for the charity auction.

She stretched, her gaze returning to the creation on the table. The box was unlike anything she'd ever done. It felt right—the piece was going in the direction she wanted it to—but at the same time it was so different she felt a bit of discomfort, as well. Where there had always been darkness, now there was light. Where there had always been mystery, now it was clear. Flipping her glasses back into place, she picked up her tweezers and nudged a sliver of mirror she'd already set in one corner to the left a quarter inch.

What would Sarah say?

Anise didn't have to think too hard to hear her friend's voice.

"What do you think you're doing, Anise? This is appallingly mundane. Where's your energy? Where's the provocation? This looks like something you'd find in a gift store, for God's sake.

"Where's your edge?"

The words echoed loudly and Anise's fingers began to tremble as she second-guessed herself. But she continued. She was working from the heart, just as she always did. If Sarah didn't like it, that was too bad. The realization hurt Anise—her friendship with Sarah had always been important to her—but she didn't understand Sarah's attitude toward Bishop. Why didn't she like him? Their conversation the other day had Anise beginning to question things she'd never thought about before. As a result, the closeness she and Sarah had always shared had begun to feel a little too stifling.

In a sharp contrast she couldn't ignore, Bishop's attitude last night had loosened the bricks in the wall Anise used to protect herself. His total acceptance of who she was was making her feel free in a way she never had before.

She paused, her tweezers hovering over the box as she remembered the way he had touched her hair. Letting the moment play out, she imagined his lips on hers, his hand on her back. What would it have felt like if he'd continued? What kind of lover would Bishop be? A slow one, she decided.

A slow, deliberate one who would be as concerned about her satisfaction as he was about his own, if not more so. A thoughtful one. A good one.

She shook her head to dislodge the thoughts. Her work meant everything to her and she wanted to concentrate on it. She didn't want someone special in her life, no matter how good he made her feel.

She had everything she needed.

Didn't she?

IT WAS THE END OF THE DAY before Bishop made his way down to the fourth floor to the computer lab. When he pushed open the double doors, Tony, the tech he'd seen earlier, greeted him with a file folder in his arms. "We printed all the e-mails just in case," he said, holding up the folder. "But we're finished with the drive. We made a duplicate so you can go through it if you like. I stuck it on one of our test machines in the back. We went ahead and locked up the original. You wanna look at these or check out the machine itself?"

"I'd rather see the machine."

Tony nodded. "Knock yourself out. It's the one next to the door."

Bishop said his thanks as he started for the rear of the lab. Five minutes later he was deep into the contents of Kenneth Capanna's e-mails.

Five minutes after that, he hit pay dirt.

The e-mail from Brittany was short and to the point.

i know your not going to pay attention to this but i need more money for everything thats going on at school and i don't care what you think because its the truth You dont have a clue about what stuff costs now and you dont care either all you care about is your own life and what your doing but its important to me. id be better off if you were dead. me and mom would both be better off I hate you your the worst father in the world

Bishop whistled softly. The childish threat, filled with misspellings and grammatical errors, was probably nothing more than just that—a childish threat—

but the rage he'd seen the girl display during her argument with Anise had to be considered as well. She was carrying around a load of anger. People couldn't contain that kind of burden forever, no matter how hard they tried.

He scanned the rest of the e-mails but he found nothing different. Most of the remaining notes from the teenager were along the same lines, either asking for money or berating her dad. Despite knowing he shouldn't, Bishop found himself feeling even sorrier for the kid than he had before.

Kenneth's remaining e-mails were mainly from Robin about work. He had a few from clients, a few others from friends, but that was it.

Bishop turned to the other files on the computer. The majority of them were Excel documents from the accounts of Capanna's various clients, including Anise. When Bishop saw her name, he didn't hesitate to open the file and look at the bottom line.

Her income was impressive. And so was her tax bill.

Until his junior year, Bishop had majored in accounting at the University of Miami. He'd switched to criminal justice after realizing how bored he was with numbers, but he knew his way around a spreadsheet. After a couple of false starts, he followed the paper trail spread out before him.

Then he did it again.

An hour later, he sat back in disbelief.

For at least one year, possibly two, Kenneth Capanna had been flipping funds over faster than an Olympic gymnast doing a floor routine. From one account to another, back and forth, every way but sideways. He'd moved money in and out of private accounts without any regard to law or logic. The trail was so convoluted Bishop had to draw himself a flow chart.

Capanna's office computer had been thoroughly examined. None of these files had been on it. The purpose of the apartment became clear. Lei Wui had been right. Kenneth had used it for work. But the work he'd done on *this* computer was far different from the work he did at the office. He hadn't wanted it to be found by anyone.

The numbers showed how in exacting detail. Thousands of dollars, possibly tens of thousands of dollars, had been transferred into one account—with Robin Estes's name.

And every last penny of it had come from Anise.

Lei Wui's comment about Kenny having plenty of money shot into Bishop's mind. Kenny had it all right. It just hadn't been his own. Bishop stared at the paint-flecked wall behind the computer and shook his head, a dozen different motivations popping into his head where none had existed before.

Capanna had been stealing from Anise and was planning on blaming Robin. She found out and killed him.

Capanna and Robin were working together but he wasn't doing his part so she killed him.

Robin had been stealing from Anise, Capanna found out and she killed him.

Sarah had backed up Robin's alibi for the night of the murder, though. The only way Robin could have shot Capanna *and* been with Sarah was if she had a clone. Could Sarah have lied for her? Recalling Anise's comment, he dismissed that idea as quickly as it came. She was right. Sarah guarded Anise like a mother hen looked after her favorite chick. She'd never allow Anise to be defrauded like that. If she knew.

Then again, maybe the whole thing was a coincidence.

Robin and Kenneth could have been stealing from Anise for years. Capanna's death could have had nothing to do with their embezzling but realizing the scheme was about to come unraveled, Robin could have freaked when Kenneth had been randomly killed. That would explain her appearance at Anise's house the other night. She hadn't known what to do next so she'd panicked.

He wasn't too sure he knew what to do, either.

CHAPTER TEN

BISHOP LEFT his office and headed straight for Robin Estes's apartment. He knocked on her door but no one answered. The neighbor was nowhere to be seen, either. The apartment manager informed him she had six hundred apartments with over two thousand residents. She didn't notice who came and went. Robin's rent for the month was paid and that's all she knew. And apparently cared about.

He sat in the parking lot and tried to decide what to do. His phone rang once. Donna Capanna was on the other end. With an attitude he didn't much care for, she informed him he could speak with Brittany the following Wednesday at their home. Their family attorney would not be available before then. They hung up with neither one of them looking forward to the meeting. He went back to his thinking, Anise's face haunting him, the image of her clear blue eyes and perfect skin refusing to fade. He knew it wasn't the right thing to do, but he wished he'd kissed her the other night. He should have ignored his good sense and done what he wanted. Getting it out of his system might be the only cure. He stared at Robin's front door and told himself he was in deep trouble. Twice he picked up his phone and started to call Anise, but twice he forced himself to stop. He didn't want to tell her what he'd found out about Robin and the money until he understood it better himself. And that meant talking to Robin.

Tuesday came and went but Robin didn't appear. Wednesday proved to be a repeat. Thursday night, dressing for the charity dinner, Bishop acknowledged the truth; he couldn't wait any longer. He had to discuss the missing funds with Anise and gauge her reaction.

But not tonight.

Tonight he didn't want to think about

the case, or why he shouldn't be going out with Anise in the first place, or any of the countless other arguments that existed for him not getting any closer to her than he already was. He only wanted to think about her, official policy be damned. Bishop pulled up outside Anise's house half an hour later. Her porch light came on then the door opened and she stepped out. He met her halfway up the sidewalk, his breath catching inside his chest.

The hem of her filmy white dress floated around her ankles like a low-lying cloud, the halter top showing off her shoulders. She carried a gold gift box in one hand and a small white purse in the other. Her hair was pulled back in a loose bun and all he could think about was undoing it and running his hands through its silkiness.

She said his name—for the second time, he realized a moment too late—and looked at him with a puzzled frown. "Is something wrong?"

"Only with my eyes," he confessed. "I've never seen an angel flying this close to the ground."

She laughed and made a face, then hit him on the arm with her purse. "Oh, now you're getting all corny on me! Please... I can't stand it."

He laughed, too, but he could see she was pleased by the compliment. Under the blush she'd stroked on her cheeks, a deeper pink developed, and that one was for real. How could he have ever been suspicious of someone who looked like her?

He led her to the car and opened the door with a gallant gesture. She gathered her skirt and climbed inside, the box clutched to her breasts protectively.

He went to the other side, started the engine, then jutted his chin toward her hands. "Is that your piece?"

"Yes. I just finished it this evening." She grimaced and shrugged. "It was done but at the last minute I decided to change something. I'm surprised I managed to get dressed in time."

"Can I see it?"

"Not yet," she said. "When we get there, okay?"

He nodded, although he didn't really

understand, and told her about the past few days. "I don't want to talk about the case tonight," he said, "but I know you're curious so I'll tell you right now, there's been no trace of Robin. She hasn't been back to her apartment and no one has seen or heard from her."

"I wonder where she went? And why she left?"

Bishop was pretty sure he could answer the second question but he kept that information to himself. "Who knows?" he said lightly. "She'll turn up sooner or later, but we don't have to worry about that for the next few hours."

The Museum of Fine Arts came into view twenty minutes later. On the edge of downtown, the building hosted the charity event every year. Bishop pulled out his Official Business placard and parked by the curb. Taking Anise's arm, he led her up the broad steps and inside the doors.

Moving through the crowd was slow going. He knew everyone associated with the charity and they knew him. Finally, they approached the area where he'd staged the silent auction. He looked down at Anise to judge her reaction.

She ran her gaze up and down the tables and her eyes widened in surprise, just as he'd hoped.

"Oh, my gosh..." She looked up at him in shock. "I had no idea this was such a big deal, Bishop! Why didn't you tell me? My God, you got someone to donate a car? And isn't that Drayton McLane over there? How did you get the owner of the Astros to show up?"

"He donates a box at Reliant Stadium every year for at least one game," Bishop replied. "We have a lot of support in the community for the club. Thank God!" He pointed to the center of a table on their right. "That's where your piece goes."

She glanced at the spot he indicated. On top of the table, an acrylic pedestal, with a spotlight on it, sat empty. "I copied Sarah's setup," he explained. "I figured she knew what she was doing at the gallery so I thought it'd work here. I changed it a bit, though. I wanted something lighter." He shrugged, feeling silly again. "Her black setup just didn't seem to fit here."

Anise's fingers went to her throat and he could see that she was touched. Then he looked closer. She seemed stunned. "How... how did you know?" she asked.

"Know what?"

"The piece I made for the auction...it's completely different from what I usually do. The way you've got the display arranged couldn't be more perfect."

BISHOP'S EYES MET Anise's and he seemed to hold her gaze. "I didn't know," he said. "I just did what I wanted to do. I made it fit you, not the art."

She shook her head in disbelief, then decided the stress of the past few days was catching up with her. Bishop didn't know about the box and the setup meant nothing. She was acting like an *artiste,* thinking the world revolved around her.

Without another word, she walked to the table and put her purse down, placing the gold box in front of her. Lifting the lid, she pushed aside the cotton padding she'd used for protection and removed the shadow box. Setting it on the platform, she pulled the catch with her fingernail and opened it up.

Standing beside her, Bishop held his breath. She waited for him to exhale, which he finally did, then she found herself waiting to breathe. What did he think?

As if he'd heard her question, he answered. "My God, Anise. It's…amazing."

She followed his stare to the creation sitting before them, the noise of the swelling crowd fading behind them. She usually worked with larger boxes. This one was a tiny perfect square. Two inches on every side. Instead of obscuring the glass, she had lined it with mirrors and filled it with light. Everything in it glittered, sending reflections back to the beholder. A rainbow of pale greens and blues made from marble fragments and sea glass covered the bottom in a way that managed to be both patterned and random. Curving up the side, the color held the viewer's attention. Slowly the eye noticed the other elements. A fleck of silver here, a spot of gold there, a tiny heart buried at the bottom, under a glaze of powder.

"I think it turned out pretty well," she said simply.

He blinked and pulled his gaze from the box to stare at her. "'Pretty well?'" he repeated. "Are you crazy?" He looked back at the box, speaking almost as if to himself. "I never understood people who spent millions of bucks on paintings and stuff like that, but now I get it. It's not the art they want." He stared down at her. "It's how it makes you feel when you look at it. That's the secret, isn't it? That's what it's all about."

She was holding onto his arm but she had no idea when she'd taken it. "That's it," she said. "That's it, exactly. I wanted to create something—" She broke off, not sure of the word, then he supplied it.

"Hopeful," he said. "It makes you think things might be okay, after all. That maybe the world isn't falling apart, and the North Pole isn't melting, and there just might be some good in us all."

She laughed in delight. "I wasn't thinking quite that globally, but sure, why not? Whirled Peas for everyone."

He grinned. "Maybe I went a little over the top," he acknowledged, "but you know what I mean."

"Yes, actually, I do. Because that *is* what I wanted. Something positive, something bright. You're doing such great work here helping all these kids—it just seemed appropriate. I wanted to express that." She held back a bit, then took the plunge. He didn't know the significance of her revealing the box's name…but she did. "I call it *Heaven*."

He bent down and kissed her, his lips touching hers in a brief promise that left her wanting more. "That's perfect," he murmured. "And so are you."

EVERYONE THEY SAW greeted Bishop, then wanted to meet Anise. Word had spread quickly about the box and Bishop knew before they even found their seats and sat down for dinner that bidding on the shadow box would be fierce.

The chairwoman of the organization made some brief remarks, thanking everyone for their hard work, including Bishop, then she promised a lively evening with dancing to follow the auction after dinner. She concluded by reminding everyone that bids would be taken on the auction items until dessert was served. Waiters appeared quickly and Anise dug into her steak with relish.

"This is so good," she said. "I don't understand these people who won't eat meat. Give me a steak and a beer any day."

Amen, he thought. He took a drink from his wineglass and wished for a Bud. "Do you have a friend who's vegetarian? You sound like you have to put up with one."

"Sarah is," Anise answered between bites. "She's always fussing at me for eating beef. She thinks it's going to kill me."

"You and Sarah go back a long way." His statement was an observation, not a question.

"We've been inseparable since we were kids. I think I mentioned before that I lived in the house next door to the Levys until my mother died." She hesitated, the words obviously not easy to get out. "After that, I went to live with them. My mother didn't have any other family and my dad had never been in the picture."

"They adopted you?"

"Not formally," she replied. "I was their foster child according to the courts, but they treated me like a daughter."

"You were lucky."

"Very," she said. "If they hadn't come forward, I'd be one of the kids your charity is raising money for and probably homeless to boot."

"Are they still around?"

"Mr. Levy passed away ten years ago," she said. "He was over fifty when they had Sarah but her mom was a lot younger. She's in an assisted living facility. She has good days and bad."

"I didn't realize she still had family."

"I need to go see Rachel. I haven't been since the spring. She's a very special lady."

"When did Sarah start working in the gallery?"

"Believe it or not, right out of high school. She had a vision for it from the very beginning. Her parents had always featured very traditional artists and works but Sarah wanted to move in an edgier direction. It took her awhile to get started and for a few years, neither one of us was very sure she'd make it."

"But she did."

Anise sipped her wine. "She did. It's one of the premiere galleries in town now."

He tapped her wineglass with his own. "And *you* are one of the premiere artists."

Anise laughed lightly. The sound reminded him of the box waiting to be auctioned. Bright and airy and full of joy. "I wouldn't say that," she said. "I make a living, though, and that's more than a lot of artists can claim so I'm happy."

Bishop didn't change his expression but behind his mask all he could think of was the money Robin had been stealing. Anise was more successful than she knew.

"What about you?" She broke through his thoughts. "You aren't from Texas, are you?"

He made a mock face. "Oh, no. Does it show?"

"It's the accent. You don't have that deep Texas twang."

"I grew up in Florida," he said. "Just outside of St. Pete. Went to Miami U. Then headed west and joined HPD. The guys at work said I can consider myself an adopted Texan after that long."

She pushed aside her plate. "You like what you do?"

"I couldn't do anything else although I tried being an accountant while I was in college."

"An accountant? I can't imagine that."

"I couldn't, either," he said. "That's why I ended up in criminal justice."

Her fingers wrapped themselves around her wineglass. "But you like helping others, you like doing the right thing…" She waved a hand to indicate the crowd around them. "You look out for those who can't do it themselves. That's why you want Kenneth's killer. He can't speak any more so you're speaking for him." Her eyes went soft. "I think that's pretty cool."

ANISE DIDN'T KNOW who was more anxious, her or Bishop. By the time the dinner was over, they were both excited and nervous. It took forever to announce the bids for the things listed before her box, but finally the chairwoman got to it.

"Our next item is Number 29. Our chair in charge of acquisitions outdid himself on this. It's an original piece of art by Houston's own Anise Borden. A shadow box of amazing character, this incredible work contains all the elements of sophistication for which Ms. Borden's works are famous. Represented exclusively by the Levy Gallery, Ms. Borden is a nationally known artist who will be hosting a private showing at the gallery next month. We're very fortunate to benefit from her kindness this evening and bidding for this particular item was highly competitive. In fact, in a move we can only label as extremely generous, the winning bid—a record for the HPD Children's Charity in the art division—has been made via telephone. This item is going to Sarah Levy, the owner of the Levy Gallery. She will display the shadow box at Ms. Borden's upcoming show and resell it there, the gallery's profits at that time also coming back to our cause."

The crowd broke into applause, a few scattered whistles accompanying the news as well. Stunned by the announcement, Anise turned to Bishop. "Did you know about this?"

He shook his head, clapping with everyone else. "I had no idea," he said over the noise. "The people in charge must have called her when I told them you were giving something. I'm as surprised as you are."

The crowd settled down and the chairwoman continued but Anise remained in a state of shock, even after the floor was cleared and the dancing had begun. The gesture Sarah had made was a spectacular one and generous to a fault. Anyone in their right mind would have been pleased. But even as she had those thoughts, Anise found herself questioning Sarah's motive. She didn't approve of Bishop yet here she was contributing to his charity. Why did she feel so compelled to place herself in *every* part of Anise's life? A year ago—a *month*—ago, Anise wouldn't have given the act a second thought, except to be grateful, but now she wondered. What was behind Sarah's move?

Thankfully Anise didn't have too much

time to dwell on the troubling question. Bishop swept her into his arms and they began to sway to the music. The warmth of his body and the feel of his hands on her back was all that she needed. They didn't leave the dance floor for at least an hour and then it was only to grab a drink and go right back. At the end of the night, Anise climbed into Bishop's Crown Vic, feeling like Cinderella.

They rehashed every detail on the ride home, Anise unable to remember exactly how many people had come up and thanked her for her contribution.

"Oh, Bishop, I so appreciate you letting me add my box to the auction," she said as they pulled up to the curb outside her house. "I feel like I really did something good tonight."

Bishop laughed. "You did! And Sarah's move was pretty amazing, too. We have some pretty high flyers supporting us but she managed to pull that off quite well."

"I still can't believe it."

Bishop reached across the car seat and brushed a curl of hair off her neck. The touch left her tingling. His hand slipped down to her bare shoulder. "Sarah's a good friend."

"Yes, she is," Anise replied. "She can also be incredibly selfless, especially where I'm concerned."

As she spoke, Anise criticized herself for her earlier thoughts. Sarah had nothing but her good interest at heart. What had she been thinking?

"In fact, when we were kids, she saved my life," Anise said simply. "How much more generous can you get than that?"

HE'D BEEN RUBBING her shoulder with his thumb but at her words, he stopped. "What do you mean she saved your life? Are you speaking literally?"

"I am." She looked across the seat at him, the darkness hiding her expression. "I still find it hard to talk about—obviously—but my mother didn't just die when I was a kid. She was killed in a house fire. It was arson. The police never uncovered who set the fire. I survived because of Sarah. She knew exactly where I was hiding, and she ran into the house and found me."

"The firemen didn't stop her?" he asked in amazement.

"They had no idea she'd gone inside. They were spraying water on the house on one side and she went in from the other. I was in the closet. She found me, then went back out and told them where I was. She would have carried me out herself but she couldn't lift me. I'd already collapsed from the smoke. Her mother almost killed her when she found out what she'd done but she was proud of her, too. The firemen gave her a little medal and all was forgiven. Her dad was the only one who really fussed at her."

He didn't say anything but his hands slid down Anise's arm and he took her fingers in his, turning her palm over to tap the scars. He lifted her hands to his lips and kissed the roughened skin. "I wondered where these had come from," he said.

"I grabbed the doorknob to my bedroom when I was trying to get out. I couldn't even feed myself for weeks."

"I assumed they were burns," he said, "but I didn't want to ask. You're a private person."

"And you're a *perceptive* person." He could feel her eyes on his face. "Thank you for that," she said. "It's nice to have someone care who knows how to give me some room, too."

"As long as you don't want too much of it," he countered.

He was teasing but she tensed. "Actually, I need a lot of space," she said. "I have a big bubble."

"I know that," he replied. "And when it shrinks, you use your work to expand it again."

"What?"

"Don't bother to deny it. I'm the same way—or at least I used to be—so I know."

He traced the scars on her hand then let his fingers drift back up her arm. She shivered lightly but didn't pull back. "My wife left me because I worked too hard," he said. "Every time she wanted the two of us to do something, I'd find an excuse to go back to the office. This case had paperwork or that case had interviews. There was always something to be done," he said, "and if there wasn't, well...frankly, I'd make it up. I didn't want to focus on anything but my work."

"Why?"

"I thought it was important," he said. "And it was. But so is having a life. When she left me, I woke up and figured that out. That's when I realized I had to do something else. I started helping with the kids and then I got pulled into the fund-raising end of it. And I'm very glad I did. It's brought a different element into my life and expanded the way I see things."

"It's a very worthy cause."

"It's close to my heart," he said. "My dad ran out on us when I was a baby. My mom and I got by but just barely. Then my younger brother was diagnosed with leukemia. He died at four."

"Oh, Bishop…" Her words were whispered. She'd known there was a reason behind his actions but she hadn't expected something like this.

"We could have used some assistance. I like to think the kids we help now will realize that when they're grown and do the same for someone else."

"They will. You don't have to be rich to give."

"You should know," he said. "You gave a lot tonight, too."

"I enjoyed it," she said. "You made me want to do it."

"That's funny," he said, "because you make me want to do something, too."

She smiled at him, her lips going up into a slow, sensual curve. "And what might that be?"

"I think you know," he answered.

CHAPTER ELEVEN

SHE STARED AT HIM in silence and that was all the permission he needed. Bishop lowered his head and laid his lips gently on hers. Her mouth was as soft as the rest of her and he felt the world disappear, along with the car, Capanna's murder and life as he knew it. Nothing registered except the taste of Anise and the warmth of her body. For as long as he dared, he pretended nothing else mattered; then he realized he had to stop. If he didn't, the moment would take him in a direction he wasn't supposed to go.

As it turned out, he didn't have to make the painful decision. It was made for him. His phone began to ring, and he could do nothing but pull away from her and fumble for it in the darkness.

He flipped it open with one hand and answered. "Bishop."

Cody Carter was on the other end. "You got a problem," he announced.

"I got lots of problems," Bishop replied ruefully, "especially with you calling me right now. This had better be good."

"I guess that would depend on your definition of 'good.' You know someone named Robin Estes? She's a wit in the Capanna cas—"

"I know who she is." Bishop pulled away from Anise and switched the phone to his other ear. The one away from her. "She came home?"

"You could say that," Carter replied. "I'm at her apartment right now. The maintenance man went into her place this evening to spray for bugs. He found a few more than he'd been countin' on, most of 'em maggots."

A feeling of tightness started in the pit of Bishop's stomach and made its way up to his chest. "Go on."

"She was in the back bedroom with a

forty-five beside her. One shot, left temple. She's as dead as they get. You better come over here."

ANISE DIDN'T NEED to ask. She could tell by Bishop's body language their magical night was over. The carriage had just turned back into a pumpkin.

"I have to go," he said shutting his phone with a snap. "I'm sorry, Anise, but this is how it works."

"I understand," she said. "Is…is everything okay?"

"Not really." He opened his door then slammed it shut and came to her side of the car. Walking to her door, he was a million miles away.

But he took the time to check out her house. He came back into the living room where he'd told her to wait. "Everything's fine here," he said. "I'll call you when I can."

At the front door, he stopped, his eyes meeting hers for the barest of moments. "I really enjoyed our evening," he said. "Forgive me for ending it so abruptly?"

"It's not a problem." And it wasn't. The

intimacy they'd shared only a few minutes ago in the car already seemed like too much. Pulling back from him, physically and emotionally, she opened the door. "I understand."

He looked down at her as if reading her mind; her relief must have been obvious. She thought he might comment on it, then he seemed to realize he didn't have the time. Kissing her until she couldn't breathe, he ran out the door a second later.

BISHOP HAD BEEN inside Robin Estes's apartment for three hours. In addition to the tech guys, Carter, the responding officers and some others, a couple of print reporters had shown up as well. They'd hung around until it'd become clear they were getting nothing for the morning edition. The television people hadn't bothered to come out. Just another death in the big city for them. If Bishop was really lucky, the murder might not make the local news until the following evening, if that. He didn't want Anise to learn about the shooting until he could tell her himself but he couldn't call her yet.

Because he had no idea just what he *would* tell her. Robin Estes had been shot but the who, why and how of it were as much of a mystery as they'd been when he'd walked in the door. No one in any of the surrounding apartments had heard or seen her return, including the uniforms he'd had driving by. Where had she been since leaving Anise's house? When had she returned? He didn't have any answers.

For that matter, he wasn't sure he understood who Robin Estes had even been in life. Her home projected the same personality she'd shown when he'd met her at Kenneth Capanna's office. Bland, blah and boring. The furnishings were basic Ikea, her decorating straight out of the box. Nothing in the place revealed even a hint of the woman herself. Inside the drawer of her nightstand where he usually struck gold, he only found a photograph of her with Sarah, a recent birthday card from Madelyn Sutcliff and a charcoal drawing of a dog, nothing else. He took the photo and tucked it in his pocket. A quick search of her desk and the rest of the place turned up even less.

Her suitcases were inside her closet. If she'd planned a trip or gone anywhere, she'd come home and emptied the bags.

He went into the bedroom. The M.E. assistants were in the process of moving the body; they'd estimated her time of death as sometime earlier in the day, midafternoon maybe. She'd already been dead when he'd been knocking on her door. A vague wash of guilt hit him before he told himself to stop acting stupid. He couldn't have known.

Standing quietly, he watched the men do their job. He'd had a case once where he'd found a suicide note under the body but this time, Bishop had no such luck. There was nothing on the carpet but the bloody stain she'd made when she'd shot herself.

He did, however, have the gun.

It was an M1911. A .45 semiautomatic with a five-inch barrel. Seven in the magazine and one in the chamber.

It was the same kind of weapon that had taken Kenneth Capanna's life.

HER HEAD STILL SPINNING from the night before, Anise called Sarah early the following morning. She wanted to atone for her suspicious thoughts even though Sarah had no idea she'd indulged in them.

"You're a very bad friend!" she said when Sarah answered the phone.

"And why is that?"

"You should have told me you were going to bid on the box I made for the HPD Children's Charity event! I was so shocked when they made the announcement I nearly fell out of my chair."

"I can be generous when I want to," Sarah said with mock indignation.

"That's not what I meant." Anise laughed. "I was impressed, that's all. It was a very sweet gesture and I was touched. You're going beyond the call of duty. Especially since I know how you feel about Bishop."

"Bishop hasn't got anything to do with this. I wanted to make the most of the opportunity, that's all."

"Well, you certainly did. Everyone there was quite impressed." Anise dropped her voice. "Including me. It really was a nice thing for you to do, Sarah, and I do appreciate it."

The other woman sounded pleased when she answered. "I'm glad it made you happy. That's all I've ever wanted to do, Anise. You're a very special person—a special friend—and sometimes I forget to tell you that. I guess this was a way for me to express that sentiment. And prove a point."

Anise could tell Sarah's compliment came straight from the heart but she found herself wishing she'd left off the codicil. It was always that way with Sarah, though, and Anise realized her anxiousness probably stemmed from that. Ever since she'd been a child, Sarah had had a hidden motive for everything she did, and that included the buying of Anise's box. Nothing was ever simple with her.

"And what might that point be?" Anise pressed.

"I don't have time to go into it right now. I have to be at the caterer's around eleven. The one I've hired for your show. Why don't you come with me and we'll go have lunch afterward and I'll explain."

"Oh, Sarah, I couldn't care less what we have to eat. You decide."

"No. I want everything to be perfect and perfect means you're happy with the details. This is going to be your big day," Sarah replied. "You need to help plan it."

She wanted to work but still feeling guilty, Anise agreed. "I'll go," she said. "As long as I get to pick where we eat lunch."

Sarah sighed heavily. "All right. You can pick this time."

They hung up, Anise appreciating Sarah's gesture but wishing all the while that her friend had asked about her evening, too. She wanted to talk about the party, about what she'd worn and how Bishop had looked, and the way he'd kissed her right before he'd left. She wanted to share how she felt about him, but she couldn't. Not with Sarah.

All Anise could do was sit and stare out the window and go over the evening in her mind. Bishop had surprised her last night, especially his reaction to her piece. He'd truly been impressed…and touched. She'd heard the sincerity in his voice and seen it in his eyes. To realize she'd created something that powerful had made the evening even more special.

And Bishop even more appealing.

Letting her mind wander in that direction, she wasted half the morning before heading out to the gallery.

Sitting in the dining room of Luther's two hours later, she watched Sarah shake her head as she picked at her salad. "I swear, Anise, you look like someone who would only eat at the finest places yet you choose a dive like this? They don't serve food here. This is garbage."

"I love barbecue." Anise took a bite of her sandwich and wiped her mouth with her napkin. Deciding she'd been too quick to judge, she tested Sarah. "Beef is good for you. We had wonderful steaks last night at the Museum. Those guys know how to throw a ball, that's for sure."

Sarah nodded absentmindedly, the bait ignored, either deliberately or not, Anise couldn't tell. "What did you think about the caterer?"

Disappointed but not surprised, Anise answered. "She's fine." She glanced at her watch. She still hadn't heard from Bishop and she would have thought he would have called her by now.

"Just fine? Not superb?"

"As you just pointed out ever so politely, I'm not a gourmand." Anise held up her dripping sandwich. "This is the kind of stuff I eat."

"Do you think we should get someone else? If you weren't pleased with what we tasted, I can keep searching. There are lots of people out there."

Anise looked at Sarah in exasperation. "I'm sure she'll impress all the clients and they'll be so thrilled with the food they'll buy more boxes." Anise picked up her iced tea glass. "What do you want me to say? It's food. It was good. I don't care."

Sarah put down her knife and fork and stared at Anise, her eyes narrowing. "What's up? You aren't paying attention at all. And why do you keep staring at your watch?"

"I'm expecting a call from Bishop," she admitted. She'd told Sarah about the apartment and the computer on the way to the caterer's office. "I would have thought he'd know more about the e-mails by now. He said he'd let me know."

Anise braced herself but instead of lashing out with the sharp retort she expected, Sarah spoke in a low and thoughtful voice. "Look, I know you went to the charity thing with him and I understand you're anxious about everything that's happened, but I don't think hanging on to every word he says is such a good idea."

"I am *not* hanging on to every word—"

Sarah held up a hand. "You said you thought he was nice, but I'm getting the feeling this might be more serious than 'nice.' Are you…falling for this guy?"

"Oh, for goodness' sake, Sarah, c'mon! How could I be 'falling' for him? You're misinterpreting the situation entirely."

"Am I?" She took a sip of the wine she'd ordered to go with her salad. "Or are you?"

"What's that supposed to mean?"

"I've been thinking about it." Sarah pushed her salad to one side, then leaned her elbows on the table, her expression intense. "He's obviously appealing to you and I believe you should figure out why."

"Something tells me I don't need to," Anise retorted. "I think you've done that for me."

Undeterred, Sarah continued. "You never had a father. This guy appears when you're vulnerable, he's sympathetic, he's an authority figure, he's big and strong and saves you from Robin. You told me you weren't getting involved with anybody else but you went out with him…." She shrugged and leaned back. "I think you should consider the implications."

"Yeah, well, the other night you told me you weren't my mother. What changed?"

Sarah grinned, Anise's jab delivered in such a sweet voice she couldn't do anything else.

"I lied," she said with a laugh. "I *am* your mother, and your sister, and your best friend, and your manager." Her voice deepened. "I don't want to see you hurt. To me, this guy looks like someone who could do that. You don't know anything about him, but I can tell you're interested in him and I'm worried, that's all. I don't want you to get blindsided again. Kenneth was a disaster. It's good for your art, but why take a chance on repeating that kind of agony?"

Anise wanted to tell Sarah she was right. But she couldn't. Something about Bishop was drawing her in. She felt the need to understand him like she would a puzzling piece of art. She wanted to dissect him and see what made him so special, so different. She wanted to analyze him, piece by piece.

She lifted her eyes. Without any warning, the minor irritation Anise had felt earlier shifted into uneasiness. Sarah's eyes were filled with a disapproval that far outweighed her spoken opinion. Her expression changed as soon as their gazes met, but the message had been delivered.

Thankfully Sarah turned the conversation back to the show and they finished their lunch. Anise told herself Sarah had her best interests at heart; she owed Sarah so much and all the other woman wanted in return was their friendship. How could Anise be so ungrateful, she thought as they stepped out into the parking lot. She turned and hugged Sarah.

"Thanks for being such a good friend,"

Anise said. "I know you're trying to protect me."

Sarah hugged her back. "All I've ever wanted for you was the best," she said. "Remember in the fourth grade when Miss Barnes put your drawings up in the back of the room?"

Anise laughed. "How can I forget? You snuck in during recess and took them all down. When we came back in, you'd hung them in the front. The chalkboard was covered. You had a fight with Lucy Johnson over it, too, as I recall. She thought if anyone's pictures should be front and center, hers deserved the spot."

"Lucy was a moron and your drawings were great!" Sarah said in mock distress. "They deserved the place of honor!" Her expression shifted. "That's all I want for you now, too. I want to show the world what a fantastic artist you are and protect you from anyone who doesn't see that brilliance. If I get too enthusiastic, I'm sorry."

"I understand," Anise said. "And I appreciate it, I really do. And I like the caterer. I thought the food was great. Thanks for tending to the details."

Sarah beamed. "It's going to be the best show ever, Anise. I have something special planned for you, too, but don't ask for any hints because I'm not giving them. You'll love it, though."

They went their separate ways after saying goodbye but instead of starting her car and driving off as Sarah did, Anise sat for a bit and let her mind wander. She recalled their conversation and Sarah's comments about Bishop. Then Anise realized they'd never discussed Sarah's plans for the box she'd bought. The thought returned Anise to the events of the evening before. It had been so special.

When her cell phone rang a second later, Bishop's exhausted voice came over the line. "I need to talk to you," he said without preamble. "Where are you?"

She told him her location, then asked, "Why? What's wrong?" Halfway kidding, she added, "You sound like you just pulled an all-nighter."

"I did," he said. "And the news isn't good."

CHAPTER TWELVE

"IT'S ROBIN," he said. "She's been shot."

Anise was glad she was already sitting down. Her free hand gripped the steering wheel, her knuckles going white. "Oh, my God, Bishop! What happened? Is she okay?"

"There's a Starbucks two streets south of where you are. I'll be there in ten minutes. Let's talk there."

Putting her car in gear, Anise made her way to the coffee shop but she wasn't sure how. One minute she was at Luther's and the next she was sitting in Starbucks, waiting for Bishop. He strode inside a little later, wearing his tux pants and shirt from the night before, his jaw shadowed, his eyes bleary. Despite the fact that he looked bone-tired and heartsore, Anise felt a tingle of desire, his barely disguised anger making him all the more attractive. He was upset because he cared.

He came to her side and kissed her hard, as if bracing her for his news. A few moments after, with coffee cups in hand, they sat back down. Anise wrapped her fingers around the paper cup. It was ninety-five in the shade but she was chilled.

"Is she—?"

"She's dead." He took a sip of his coffee and looked over the cup. "The gun was beside her."

Anise's heart took an extra beat. "Oh, no! Suicide? Are you sure?"

"No. I'm not sure but it looks that way."

Closing her eyes in disbelief, Anise felt him put his hand on top of hers.

"I'm sorry." He spoke quietly. "This is why I had to leave last night but I couldn't say anything until I knew what was going on. I hope you understand."

"Of course." She opened her eyes and shook her head. "Bishop, I can't believe this...."

"Do you know how to contact her family?"

"I don't have any numbers for them, but I'll call Sarah. She might."

He nodded, then paused, regret on his face. Anise didn't want to ask, but she had to. "What else?"

"I found out something the other night when I got into Kenneth's computer. I wanted to talk to Robin before I spoke to you about it but now that's not going to happen."

Anise stiffened her shoulders. "What is it?"

"They were stealing from you," he said bluntly. "Thousands of dollars. I found the spreadsheets on the computer."

HE FELT THE SHOCK as it rippled through her. Anise knew nothing about the money.

"Stealing from me? What do you mean?"

"For almost two years, someone's been transferring funds from the bank accounts Kenneth held for you into one with Robin's name. A lot of money. You didn't know about this, did you?"

"I don't have a clue what you're talking about. I let Kenneth and Sarah manage all my finances." She swallowed, the column of her throat moving with a jerk. "How much money are we talking about?"

"A lot," he answered. "You'll need an audit to get an exact amount but my best guess is tens of thousands. Maybe more."

She seemed unfazed by the size of the missing funds, then he realized why. Money didn't mean that much to Anise, otherwise she wouldn't have allowed other people to manage it for her in the first place. Once again, he contrasted her to everyone else he knew. And once again, she came out on top, despite the fact that her naïveté, at least in this case, had been costly. Her voice pulled him back.

"What's happening here, Bishop? What's going on? I don't understand."

His eyes met hers, the already fading memory of her body against his own a poor substitution for how good the real thing had felt when they'd danced. He'd tried to tuck the memory away so it wouldn't be tarnished by what had followed but even Robin's death had been unable to push it too far. He was definitely developing feelings for Anise that he shouldn't have.

He cleared his mind and forced himself to focus on the job. "I don't understand, either. I just hope no one else dies before I figure it out."

"You will." She spoke with more confidence than he had. "But I can't imagine what Robin and Kenneth were involved in. There's only one thing I do know for sure. Whatever it was, it wasn't sexual. It couldn't be. Robin was gay and Kenneth, well, Kenneth had Lei."

"Stranger things could happen."

"Maybe, but not in this case. Kenneth used to talk about Robin's plainness. He could be cruel sometimes, especially about things like that."

"Did he have a problem with her lifestyle? Give her a hard time about it?"

"He never said anything to her face, but behind her back, he probably did. Not to me, of course, but to others."

"Why not to you?"

"Because he knew I wouldn't put up with it. I love Sarah. We've been friends forever and I wouldn't listen to anything bad he had to say about her or her friends. I just wouldn't."

Behind the espresso machine, the teen-aged barista tapped a metal cup against the counter, the sound loud and hollow. "Do you think Robin killed Kenneth?" Anise asked quietly.

"What do you think?"

"Yesterday I would have said 'no way,' but now…" She shook her head with a helpless motion. "Now, I don't know. If she *was* stealing from me, I'd have to ask why she needed all that money. She lived simply, dressed plainly… Kenneth obviously knew what was going on since he kept the second set of books. What's your theory?"

He leaned back and rubbed a hand along his jaw. "I'm not sure I have a theory, but there are other possibilities."

"Like what?"

"Well, for one thing, we don't know for sure Robin committed suicide."

"You said the gun was right beside her."

"That's true, but that doesn't necessarily mean she used it on herself. It could have been staged. Whoever killed her could have also killed Kenneth. Maybe they had an unhappy client. I could have missed something on those spreadsheets. They might have been stealing from someone else, too." He shrugged. "Maybe it was random. She might have come home and found someone in her apartment. They might have shot her, panicked and dropped the gun, then run. Her death could be totally unrelated to Kenneth's. There's hundreds of scenarios. We just don't know which one fits right now. But we will soon enough."

ANISE CALLED Sarah before leaving Starbucks. "I have to tell you something," Anise announced when Sarah answered. "And it's not very good."

"Are you okay? What's wrong?"

"It's not about me, Sarah. This is about Robin. She's been shot. In fact, she's... dead."

"What?" Sarah's voice rose in shock. "Where? When?"

"The maintenance man at her apartment building found her last night. They aren't sure yet what happened. Bishop called me right after you and I finished eating. We're at a Starbucks near Luther's." Anise took a deep breath. "I wanted to call you as soon as I could."

"Oh…" Sarah's voice caught, then she regained control. "I don't know what to say. Does he think it's a suicide?"

Anise started to ask Sarah if she knew about the money, but she stopped. If Sarah *had* known anything about it, she would have already said something but Sarah's unexpected question took Anise off track regardless. "Why would you ask that? I didn't say anything about suicide."

Sarah's answer came without hesitation. "Robin had talked about killing herself for years," she said simply. "I just assumed that's what happened because she had threatened it countless times."

"I'll have to tell Bishop that," Anise murmured. "But why, Sarah? Why would Robin want to do something like that?"

Sarah sighed. "Robin did all kinds of drugs, Anise. That's why we broke up the first time. I don't put up with that kind of stuff and she took everything she could find. She was depressed and she self-medicated. In a very bad way..."

"Are you kidding me?" Anise felt her mouth fall open in shock. "I would never have thought that about Robin. Not in a million years."

"She wasn't who you thought she was. Robin was...a complicated person who lived behind a simple facade. Don't tell Bishop, though. It doesn't matter now."

"That's not true, Sarah! It does matter." Anise thought instantly of the missing funds. "It could explain a lot of things. I *have* to tell Bishop."

"I really wish you wouldn't."

Tension rolled down the line. Anise broke it the only way she knew how, by switching subjects. "We can discuss it later, okay? Right now, we need to tend to something more urgent. Do you have any numbers for her parents?"

"I might. I'll have to dig around a bit."

"If you can, it would help. Bishop needs to let them know and he doesn't have any way to contact them. I don't even know for sure where they live. She left Kenneth's name and number as an emergency contact at the apartment so that's not any help."

Anise could hear Sarah moving. She imagined her rummaging through her desk. "I'll get right on it. I have clients coming in, but I'll do what I can."

"Call me when you find something."

"I will."

Bishop came back to the table. He'd gotten more coffee to go but she wasn't sure the caffeine would help. He looked too weary to continue. She relayed the conversation, including Sarah's remark about suicide then, after hesitating for a second, told him what she'd said about the drugs, as well.

"That might explain a few things, including the money," he said. "Or at least part of it. Did Kenneth do drugs?"

With a start, Anise remembered the night he'd been shot. Kenneth had not been himself that night and she recalled her own questions about his behavior. She explained her suspicions, then said, "I'm beginning to think I didn't know much about him, period. How could I have been married to him and been unaware of some of these things?"

Bishop touched her cheek with his finger then dropped it. "Everyone has secrets, Anise. Be glad you don't know them all."

LATE THE FOLLOWING EVENING Anise slipped the pan of frozen lasagna into the oven and dropped her oven mitts on the counter beside the range. Behind her, Madelyn and Sarah were talking about Robin, their voices low and subdued. Anise stared out the window above the sink. She didn't want to join the discussion because she wasn't sure she'd make any sense. Her mind had been reeling from everything that had happened but overlaying each thought was the image of Bishop at the coffee shop. He worked so hard and seemed so dedicated. She hadn't thought men like that existed anymore. She knew she was letting those thoughts intrude because she'd rather deal with them than Robin's death but they were too powerful to ignore regardless.

Kenneth had been her first husband but he hadn't been her only lover. She'd experimented as much as anyone, even living with a fellow artist for a few years right out of college. Those experiences hadn't prepared her for the reaction she was having to Bishop, though. She felt connected to him in a way she couldn't define. The need to know him better was driving her and she had no control over it.

"—not what I expected. Don't you agree, Anise?"

Hearing her name but nothing more, she turned. "What?"

Sarah looked at her with irritation. "Where are you? We've been talking ever since we got here and you haven't said two words. What's wrong?"

Crossing her arms, Sarah stared suspiciously at Anise. In the past she would have explained her thoughts but Anise couldn't forget the look in Sarah's eyes when they'd had dinner and she found herself unable to speak.

Madelyn chided Sarah instantly, her voice gentle. "Now, Sarah, please... Anise is upset, just like we are. We need to be extra patient with each other."

In the silence that followed, Sarah continued to stare. Her narrowed gaze said she knew Anise was keeping secrets…and she was. She didn't know why, but she had yet to tell Sarah about the missing funds, too.

"It's okay," Anise said to Madelyn. "We're all on edge. I'm sorry, Sarah. What were you asking me?"

"We were talking about Robin's parents," she said, her mouth a tight line. "They weren't very nice when I called."

"That's awful." Anise came toward the table. "Maybe they were just upset over hearing about Robin. It's hard to be polite when the news is so horrible."

"It was more than that," she said, her expression easing. "They were nasty. I can understand why Robin was depressed if she had to live with those two when she was growing up. Her mother informed me they didn't approve of her lifestyle, they would not be having a service here in Houston and none of us were welcome to attend the one they would be having in North Dakota."

Anise shook her head. "That's too bad.

No wonder they were estranged. I can't imagine cutting yourself off from your only child." She glanced at Sarah, looking for a way to soothe her. "Your mother accepted me with open arms and I wasn't even her own daughter. I need to go see her. I haven't been since the spring."

"Don't bother. She won't know you," Sarah said. "She doesn't know me anymore. She's gotten much worse in the last few months."

Anise felt her throat catch. Rachel Levy *had* been going downhill for years but Anise had no idea her dementia had gotten that bad. "That's okay," Anise replied stoutly. "*I* know who *she* is and that's all that counts."

Madelyn made a tsking sound and agreed, her calming tones dissipating the tension in the room. Anise did her best to concentrate on the matters at hand, and by the time they finished eating dinner, things felt normal again, the women's closeness returning. The minute she closed the door behind them after they left, however, her thoughts went right back to Bishop.

BISHOP KEPT HIS APPOINTMENT with Brittany, working it into his schedule between Robin's autopsy and a meeting with his boss where he was supposed to explain how the Capanna case had managed to expand. He was sure the autopsy would prove to be the most pleasant of the three events.

The same Hispanic woman held the door of Donna's home open for Bishop. He couldn't be certain but she seemed to look at him with sympathy. He wondered briefly what it would be like to work for a woman like Capanna, then figured he probably knew. He flashed her a smile, smoothed his tie and followed her into the formal living room. Donna sat at the same place on the sofa but this time a young man in a suit sat at her side. Brittany slouched in a nearby chair, her knee hooked over one arm, her expression both bored and scared.

Donna made the introductions, her voice clipped and unhappy. "Investigator Bishop, this is Martin Chamberlain, our attorney. Martin, this is the investigator."

They shook hands, then Bishop sent his

gaze to Brittany. "You doing okay?" he asked casually.

She nodded and looked out the window behind the couch.

Bishop's attempt to explain why he needed to talk to Brittany alone fell on deaf ears. Nobody was leaving.

The meeting proceeded exactly as Bishop had thought it would. Brittany confirmed her mother's alibi. They'd had dinner that night at Grandma and Grandpa's and then they'd come home. End of story. No, she hadn't gone anywhere else afterward. Yes, she loved her father. No, she had no idea who would want him dead.

He wasn't surprised by her tale. Capanna's parents had told him the same thing when he'd talked to them earlier in the week.

Brittany answered Bishop's questions in a low monotone, her expression as closed as her manner. He got nothing...until he asked her if she had a computer. She swung her legs off the arm of the chair, her eyes flickering to the doorway as if she were considering escape.

The lawyer interrupted right on cue. "Do

you have a warrant to review her computer files, Mr. Bishop?"

"It's just a question. I don't need a warrant for that," he replied, his stare on the girl. "But even if I did, it wouldn't matter. I found messages on the victim's computer from Brittany. You and your father communicated via e-mail, right, Brittany?"

"We did sometimes," she said cautiously. "But not that much."

Bishop pulled one of the printed notes out of his pocket and handed it to her. "Did you write that?"

Donna intercepted the piece of paper before Brittany could take it. She read the threatening letter. Her face paled and she handed the e-mail to Chamberlain.

"This is nothing," the lawyer said in a dismissive voice. "Teenaged stuff. Every kid wishes their parents were dead."

"Maybe so." Bishop flicked him a look. "But not every parent ends up that way, do they?" He turned back to the girl. "Did you write the note, Brittany? If you did, I need for you to tell me so. I have to know the truth."

She held out her hand for the note but the

attorney shook his head. "You don't have to read it. You don't have to answer that, either."

She ignored him and looked at Bishop. "What's it say?"

He repeated the note the best he could remember but she interrupted him before he was half done. "I didn't write that," she said. "Someone else musta used my computer."

"Someone else?" Bishop said skeptically. "Like who?"

She shrugged. "I dunno. Maybe a friend. Sometimes I let someone crash here. They coulda done it."

"Why would one of your friends send your dad an e-mail, pretending to be you?"

She had no answer, but he didn't need one. The guilt on her face made it obvious that she'd written the note and threatened to kill her father.

He quizzed her about talking to Anise but she denied that conversation as well, answering his questions despite the attorney's attempts to keep her silent.

"I went over there," she admitted, "but I didn't ask her about money or a will or anything. Why would I?" She rolled her eyes to indicate the house. "Does it look like anybody's starvin' around here?"

"People want money for a lot of different reasons," Bishop replied.

"Maybe so," she said. "But not me."

He switched gears again. "Where were you night before last?"

"Right here," she said, obviously without thinking. "Watching TV. It was the last episode of *24*. Why?"

He didn't bother to answer. It'd been a long shot anyway. He seriously doubted Brittany had anything to do with her father's death, much less his secretary's.

The questions and dodges continued for another frustrating twenty minutes but after that, Bishop gave up. He had better ways to waste his time. He left, putting the kid and her mother out of his mind.

ANISE DEPARTED the house before nine the following morning. To give herself something to think about other than Bishop's kiss and the chaotic jumble of her current life, she'd decided to visit Rachel Levy.

She pulled into the parking lot of the assisted living facility half an hour later. Located off the SW Freeway between a residential neighborhood and a hospital complex, the one-story building appeared as well cared for and pleasant as always, the broad front porch, lined with rocking chairs, already filled while the air was still somewhat cool. Anise nodded to the elderly residents who nodded back but an equal number seemed unaware of her as she crossed the veranda and made her way to the front door.

The inside of the home was as inviting as the outside, the generous living room holding a series of comfortable sofas offset by a fireplace at one end and a desk at the other. The receptionist sitting behind it looked up and greeted Anise.

"Hello. Are you visiting one of our residents today?"

Anise returned her smile and introduced herself. "Yes, I'm Anise Borden. I'm here to see Rachel Levy." She bent over and signed the visitor's log spread open on the desk.

"Of course, Miss Borden. I've seen you

before. Do you remember where her room is? If not, I can take you there."

"I know the way."

"Then I'll call and let her know you're coming."

The receptionist dialed a number then spoke softly. When she hung up, she tilted her head to the left. "Mrs. Levy is thrilled that you're here. Go right ahead."

The corridor was wide and filled with sun, skylights overhead spilling patches of blue sky on the carpet. Sarah had selected the home herself but Anise had approved entirely. Every time she'd visited, it seemed spotless, the residents happy. One of the features she liked the best were the niches built into the walls up and down the hallway beside each door. She knew their purpose was to help the residents find their rooms but they added a homey touch, too. Most of them held family photographs. It was hard not to stop and stare at each compelling display.

Anise found herself standing in front of one that held a black-and-white snapshot of two little girls squatting beside a lopsided sand castle, their buckets and play shovels spread before them. In the background, a swell of surf edged away from them. Standing over them was a woman in an old-fashioned two-piece bathing suit. She was shielding her eyes from the sun with her hand as she looked into the camera.

Anise's gaze blurred. She remembered the day Abe Levy had snapped the picture as if she'd just stepped out of the water. She was still staring at it when the door beside her opened.

Sarah's mother stood on the threshold. She looked exactly as she had the last time Anise had seen her. Her floral-print dress was starched and ironed, her hair curled and sprayed. She wore the same low heels Anise had seen on her feet for what seemed to be a hundred years and they were highly polished, her legs encased in gleaming stockings.

Her eyes flicked vacantly, then she broke into a smile. "Anise! My sweet Anise!"

CHAPTER THIRTEEN

THEY FELL into each other's arms and held on tightly, Anise cursing herself for having let so much time slip past since she'd visited last. She pulled back and stared in amazement at the older woman. Sarah's warning had left Anise expecting a much different reception but Rachel knew who she was. Anise was so pleased she didn't bother to wonder about the inconsistency. She hugged the woman again, then let her go. "You look wonderful, Rachel!"

"Well, why shouldn't I?" She pulled Anise into her sitting room and closed the door behind them. "I have a new doctor and he knows his stuff." Her eyes sparkled. "Maybe you should meet him, no? Sarah told me about your Kenneth, I'm so sorry, but life goes on, Anise. You're a young woman. You can't lock yourself up forever. After Abe died, I wanted to die, too, but you can't let yourself think of those things. Put the sadness out of your mind."

They sat down side by side on the small couch that rested against one wall. "I'm okay, Rachel, really. You remember, I told you that Kenneth and I were divorcing anyway."

"Ah, yes." She touched her head with the heel of her hand and made a face. "I can't recall things like I should but I'm telling you the truth, regardless. You need someone in your life. Don't wait too long!"

An image of Bishop came into Anise's mind. Rachel narrowed her gaze and grabbed her arm. "Wait a minute! You haven't been sitting around lonely, have you? You've already found someone you like. I can see it in your eyes!"

Anise opened her mouth to deny Rachel's claim.

"Don't lie to me," the older woman said before she could speak, her finger wagging in Anise's face. "I can see it! I know these things. Tell me about him."

Laughing out loud, Anise replied. "You haven't lost your touch, have you, Rachel? You can still read me perfectly."

"You're an open book, Anise. You always have been." Her eyes clouded briefly. "Sarah, now she's another matter, but you? You, I could always tell when you had a secret. So don't try and distract me. Tell me about your man."

He wasn't her man, Anise explained, but Rachel was nodding before Anise could even finish her description of Bishop.

"He's a good one," she pronounced. "A responsible one. I can tell. Policemen are special people. They care about helping others. You should hang on to him, Anise. You need someone to care about you."

Anise laughed again. "He's not mine to hang on to, Rachel! And besides that, Sarah doesn't like him. He may not stick around for long once she butts in!"

Rachel's gaze darkened again. "What do you mean? Tell me."

Anise flinched, her casual comment un-intended. For all her loving ways, Rachel and Abe had been hard on Sarah when she and Anise had been growing up. Sarah had been the one from whom they'd expected perfection. She'd usually delivered but the price had been steep.

"I'm teasing," Anise said. "You know Sarah."

Rachel drilled her with a look Anise had little trouble recalling. As a child, she'd hated to be on the receiving end of it, though that had rarely happened. "Yes, I do and for that reason, I'm asking."

Anise shrugged, wishing she could take her words back but knowing she couldn't. "You know how she is, Rachel. She loves me and she wants the best, that's all. Sometimes we don't see eye to eye about things. Since Kenneth was killed, everyone's been under a lot of stress. She thinks Bishop isn't good enough for me."

Rachel yanked her hands from Anise's and stood abruptly. "Would you like some tea, sweetheart?"

Her reaction seemed strange, but Anise wasn't surprised. Even when she had been a younger woman, Rachel could swing in and out of conversations and topics with a dexterity that left others dizzy.

"That would be nice," Anise said.

Rachel led her out of the room and down the hall. They entered a sunroom filled with plants and blooming flowers. In the center was a silver cart manned by a young woman in a pristine uniform. "We'll have two teas, Debra," Rachel pronounced, "and some of those raspberry petit fours, if you have them. This is my friend, Anise."

"Nice to meet you, miss." Nodding at Anise, the attendant spoke pleasantly. "And, Miss Rachel, don't you worry, we have your favorites. You go sit in your spot and I'll bring 'em right to you."

Rachel headed without hesitation to a quiet area in one of the corners. Anise followed her and they sat down once more. Before they could resume their conversation, the young woman appeared with two china cups and a plate of small pastries. She disappeared and Rachel spoke as if they'd never been interrupted.

"I'm worried about her."

It took Anise a second to understand. "You're worried about Sarah?"

Rachel sipped her tea, then nodded. "I think she's in love again."

Anise blinked in surprise. Sarah had said nothing to her about a new person in her life, but then again, she rarely did. "I didn't know she was seeing anyone," she said carefully.

Rachel's answer came out sharp. "I said 'I think.' I'm not certain."

"Well, if she is, wouldn't that be a good thing?"

Rachel placed her teacup on the table beside them. "I'm her mother, Anise. I love her like no one else in the world but Sarah's life is not the one I would have chosen had I been able. It isn't an easy one. She's had problems. She hasn't always handled them well." She paused, her face creased with emotion. "Even when she was a child, things were harder for her…."

"I know that, Rachel, but she's successful, she has her own business, she has a beautiful home. I think she's very happy with the way things are. She wouldn't want to change."

"You don't understand."

Anise leaned forward and put her hand on Rachel's. "I know she's been hurt," she said softly. "I know there are people who don't approve of her lifestyle, who don't appreciate the fine person she is but—"

"No. You don't understand," Rachel interrupted, "and you never will. You haven't walked in her shoes but I know things…" Her voice faded as she looked around the room. "I know things she's done. Bad things. She falls in love and nothing else matters to her. She begins to obsess. It's like she vanishes into a tunnel and there's no way out. Then she does things she shouldn't. I had always prayed it wouldn't come to this after the fire, but I knew it would. I should have known…." She began to cry silently, tears rolling down her cheeks.

Anise's heart felt tight and she reached out to pat Rachel's arm. "Oh, Rachel, we've all done things we probably shouldn't have. No one is perfect—"

"She's my daughter," she repeated. "She's my life. But you need to be careful,

Anise." She grasped Anise's hands between her own, her nails as sharp as her warning. "You need to keep a watch. Love can be a terrible, terrible thing."

Anise stared at the older woman beside her but before she could speak, Rachel's eyes widened unexpectedly and she flung out her arm, knocking over her cup and the plate of cakes. Hot tea splattered over the sofa and dripped down onto the rug beneath them. Anise yelped in surprise, then jumped to her feet. The attendant rushed to her side.

"I've got it," she said soothingly, a small towel in her hand. She blotted the stain spreading over the cushions. "Not to worry, not to worry. You're okay, Miss Rachel. Nothing's wrong. See? The tea didn't even get on your pretty dress. You're just fine."

Rachel blinked and started to mutter. Anise leaned over to take her arm, but she snatched it away. "What are you doing?" she cried.

Speechless, Anise looked down at her. "I—I'm just trying to help—"

"Now, Miss Rachel, mind your manners, okay? Miss Anise is trying to make things better."

Confusion fluttered in Rachel's gaze, then, as if it was too much to deal with, she looked away. The attendant caught Anise's eye.

"Maybe you should leave now," she suggested quietly. "Once an accident like this happens, it's hard to get them settled back down."

"But everything was perfectly all right! We were talking and then—"

The attendant's face filled with sympathy at Anise's troubled response. "That's how it goes," she answered. "They're with you one minute, then gone the next. She'll be fine, though, I promise. In an hour, she won't even remember you were here. We see it all the time." She patted Anise's arm just as she had patted Rachel's. "She'll be just okay, I promise. You run on, now."

THE VISIT WITH RACHEL left Anise rattled. Sarah's mother had seemed perfectly lucid when Anise had first gotten there. What had happened to trigger her downside?

She went over the conversation as she drove home, replaying it the best she could. By the time she pulled into her driveway, she came to the conclusion she simply didn't know. But an uneasiness she didn't like hung over her. Rachel had been trying to warn her about something and Anise didn't understand what it could have been.

Walking inside, she dropped her purse on the table by the entry, then made her way into the kitchen. She didn't have much of an appetite but it was almost noon so she fixed herself a sandwich.

Rachel had been a kind and loving substitute for the mother Anise had lost but she'd always been aware of the fact that that was all Rachel could be. She wasn't Anise's real mother and she never could be. Sarah was Rachel's daughter and that had been both a burden and a blessing for them both. Sarah had had "issues," as Rachel had sometimes put it. A difficult child, she'd been quick to anger and slow to forgive but using her cleverness, she managed to slip out of any punishment arising from her escapades.

Anise shook her head. Her appearance had obviously disturbed Rachel and she wished now that she hadn't gone. As usual, Sarah had been right. Anise should have stayed home.

She took her dishes to the sink, then went down the hall to her studio. Losing herself in her work, she cut off all thought of anything else. When she looked up, hours later, dark had fallen outside the window. She caught her reflection in the glass and was startled by the ghostly image. She let out a shaky laugh, rose from her chair and began to drop the shades.

Walking back down the hall, she headed for her bedroom. She knew from experience that the ache between her shoulders wouldn't go away without a hot shower. She'd take care of it first, then grab something to eat.

Standing just inside her closet, she shed her clothes, picked up her robe and started for the bathroom, slipping her arms inside the sleeves and belting it as she walked. At the threshold to the hallway, however, she stopped, the hair on the back of her neck rising. She told herself she was being silly but the feeling persisted.

Someone was staring at her.

She could feel their eyes on her skin as surely as if they were touching her. Her mouth went dry as she turned toward the windows in her bedroom. They faced her backyard. As usual, the blinds were down but not completely shut.

Bishop's words of caution shot into her mind.

She took a single step back into the room, her hand going to her throat as something white moved just outside the window closest to her. Trying to act as if she'd forgotten to turn out the light, she raised her other hand and flicked off the wall switch. Shadows filled the room but outside, a faint light drifted over the fence from the street lamp on the corner.

The outline of a person was framed by the window.

ANISE'S VOICE WAS LOW and controlled but the minute Bishop answered the phone, he knew something was wrong.

"Where are you?" she asked.

"The office."

"Can you come over here?" she asked. "I think…I think I need some help."

"Should I send a car?"

"No," she responded. "It's not that urgent." He heard her swallow. "But I need you. I just saw someone looking in my window."

Already striding down the hallway, the phone trapped behind his shoulder and ear, he punched the elevator buttons. "I'm going to lose you when I get in the elevator," he warned.

"It's okay," she answered. "And I'm okay. They ran away but I don't feel like being alone right now. I know I'm being silly but—"

"You're not being silly," he insisted. The bell dinged. "I'll be there in ten minutes."

He was there in five.

She met him at the door wearing a set of warmups. He wrapped her in his arms and spoke against her hair. "Tell me what you saw."

She pulled back shakily, her eyes wide as she pointed over her shoulder. "I was in the bedroom, getting undressed. I started out of the closet with my robe in my hands and by the time I got it on, I felt…felt like someone was looking at me. Then I cut off the light. I could see the person outside."

"Show me."

Holding his hand, she took him back to her bedroom, the smell of her perfume lingering in the air. She pointed. "There."

He went to the window. The locks were engaged. "I'm going outside," he said. "You wait here. I'll be right back."

Stopping for the flashlight he kept in the trunk of the Crown Vic, Bishop went down the sidewalk, then zigzagged between Anise's house and the neighbor's. A summer mist had begun to fall, a cross between rain and fog. Moisture lay heavy in the darkness, dripping off the leaves of the trees as he walked through the gate. Somewhere down the street, a dog barked once then stopped.

He directed the beam under the window. The ground was slightly dented, the mulch beneath the bushes depressed in two separate spots.

He checked the rest of the windows, then walked the perimeter of her lot. She had homes to the east and the west of her with a street out front. The back was bordered by an alley. He walked toward the alleyway and hoisted himself up to look over the fence. The narrow lane was deserted, just as he expected it to be.

Returning to the front porch, Bishop shook off droplets of water from his shoulders. Anise opened the door and raised an eyebrow.

"I saw footprints, but they aren't really clear," he said. "Whoever it was probably jumped the fence after you spotted him. He'd be long gone by now or I'd have a car over here." Stepping past her into the entry, he ran a hand through his hair and looked down at her. "I may call one anyway."

"Don't," she said. "I shouldn't have even phoned you but it scared me. Maybe I imagined it."

"Is that what you really think?"

She looked up at him. "No," she said. "I *really* think I saw someone standing there looking at me."

"I'm spending the night."

Her fingers flew to her throat. "Oh, no, Bishop. That isn't necessary, please. I don't need a babysitter—"

"I know that," he answered, his voice calm and relaxed. "But you were clearly frightened or you wouldn't have called me in the first place. Why not let me sleep on the couch?" He grinned unexpectedly. "I promise I'll stay there unless you'd prefer a different arrangement."

For a millisecond, something flickered in her gaze; then it was gone. He told himself it was his imagination. Breaking every rule he'd ever heard about maintaining personal distance, he put his hand on her chin and lifted her face, his voice going serious. "Let me stay, Anise."

"I can't do that."

"Why not?"

"You shouldn't have to deal with that kind of silliness. It's inconvenient to say the least and definitely not part of your job description, either. Besides, I'm a big girl. I can take care of myself."

"I'm aware of that fact," he said, "but

maybe I would *like* to take care of you. Have you considered that?"

To his surprise, she nodded. "Yes, actually I have."

It was his turn to raise an eyebrow.

"I don't want to want that," she said quietly. "Do you understand what I'm saying?"

"Yes, I do. But I don't like your conclusion. And I think you're wrong. It's okay to need someone on occasion."

She stared at him with her pale blue eyes, then reached up and hooked her hand behind his head, pulling him closer. "I think *you're* wrong," she said, "but for one tiny second, I'm going to pretend that's not the case."

Her lips closed over his a moment later.

THIS KISS WAS DIFFERENT. Bishop's hands were on her back and they brought her toward him, closing what was left of the gap between them, heat coming with the movement, desire as well. Anise knew that if she let him spend the night, he wouldn't be on the couch. He'd been teasing when he'd suggested that, but she wasn't. She couldn't have been more serious.

And she couldn't have been more afraid.

Bishop was the kind of man little girls dreamed about growing up and meeting one day. Tall, dark and handsome. Brave, kind and good. He was everything any woman would want.

But just like she'd said, she didn't want to want him. And if he spent the night she knew what would end up happening.

She *was* human, though, and for just a little while, she indulged herself, her fingers threading their way into his damp, thick hair, her breasts pushing against his chest.

She lost herself in the feel of his lips then she eased back. He followed her, his mouth asking for more before he understood. He released her reluctantly, his arms still on her shoulders.

"Go away," she whispered. "Go away before I change my mind and we both make a big mistake."

CHAPTER FOURTEEN

"THE MISTAKE WOULD BE for me to leave," he said. "And you know that."

She stepped away from him. "I'm not going to argue with you, Bishop. I appreciate you coming over here and helping me out, but I can't let you spend the night."

He waited for her to look at him. When their eyes met, he spoke. "Why are you doing this?"

"Please leave," she said.

He shook his head, then went to the door where he paused once again. "If you change your mind, will you call me?"

"I won't change my mind."

He nodded one more time then left, flicking open his phone the minute his feet hit the sidewalk. "I need two units to keep an eye on Anise Borden's house tonight," he told Carter when he answered. "I don't know what's going on, but some yahoo's been looking in her bedroom window."

"I told you to stop that," the younger cop said. "I knew you were gonna get caught."

"Ha, ha," Bishop replied. "Don't give me any grief, Carter. I've had enough for one night. Just get the uniforms over here and keep your jokes to yourself."

Cursing soundly, he hung up and drove back to the office. He was more than ready to risk his career to put Anise first but he couldn't make her want him and he knew it was wrong to even try.

A tiny voice spoke up in the back of his mind. It reminded him of how he had pushed away his ex-wife every time she'd reached out for him. *Payback's hell,* it twittered.

Striding into his cubicle twenty minutes later, he sat down and picked up the pile of reports he'd been about to dive into when he'd gotten Anise's call. The one on top had come from the weapons lab and the one underneath contained the autopsy results on Estes. He started reading, his mind still on Anise and the way she'd felt in his arms. Halfway through the first page, he stopped and flipped to the second one. When he finished it, he couldn't say he was surprised.

The gun found by Robin's body had been used to kill her. She had died with residue on her hands and burn marks on her temple.

According to the ballistics tests, the same pistol had been used to kill Kenneth Capanna.

Bishop lifted his gaze to the window across the room. Lights twinkled from office buildings all over downtown. The sight would have been beautiful if he'd noticed it, but he was thinking about two dead bodies and a single gun.

The conclusion seemed obvious: Robin Estes had killed Kenneth Capanna after embezzling money from his firm, then she had killed herself. Remorse, regret, release? Take your pick. Something had motivated her. He considered some more possibilities but a question remained that he couldn't ignore. What about her alibi?

Sarah Levy had said Robin had been with her when the shooting had occurred.

Sarah Levy had obviously lied for Robin.

Or Bishop's theory was all wrong.

The phone on his desk rang and he reached for it. The civilian who manned the reception area downstairs sounded bored when he answered.

"You got visitors," she said, her voice lazy. "Two of 'em. Lady and her lawyer. Can I send 'em up?"

"And their names are?"

He heard papers being shuffled. "Donna Capanna and Martin Chamberlain."

Bishop pursed his lips. He didn't have the capacity to be surprised anymore but what did those two want? He pushed himself away from his desk and met Kenneth Capanna's ex-wife and her attorney by the elevators five minutes later. Leading them to one of the interrogation rooms, Bishop felt his curiosity rise. He started to offer them coffee but the young lawyer spoke, his voice high and nervous.

"Mrs. Capanna has something she wants to tell you," he started, "Before she says anything, however, I want to get a few things established. The first one is—"

Donna Capanna interrupted. "The first one doesn't matter and neither do the fifteen others you want to talk about. I warned you about this in the elevator, Martin. I'm not wasting Mr. Bishop's time and neither are you." She glared at Bishop as though challenging him as well.

Bishop held his hands out. "You called the meeting," he said in an amicable way. "Take it away."

She looked him straight in the eye and did just that.

"I killed Kenneth," she said, her chin held high. "I planned it, I shot him and I lied about it afterward. I want you to arrest me right now and put me in jail."

SITTING ON A STOOL beside Madelyn's workbench, Anise watched the older woman attack the thick globe of clay before her. Kneading and twisting, she turned the hardened ball into a pliable rope that she draped over a rod to dry, her touch deft. Using a photograph as her guide,

Madelyn had been working on the commissioned piece for several months. A wealthy investor who frequented the gallery had requested it for his wife's thirtieth birthday. It was a bust of her and their only child.

"Rachel Levy's been sick for quite some time." Madelyn picked up a rag and rubbed it over her fingers. "I don't think your visit triggered the problem, Anise. You're being too hard on yourself."

Feeling restless and uneasy, Anise had knocked on Madelyn's door after Bishop had left. They'd discussed her Peeping Tom, if that's what he was, then Anise had told her friend about her visit with Sarah's mother. As usual, Madelyn had said all the right things, but her comforting words weren't working tonight. A guilty knot had lodged itself in Anise's chest and wouldn't go away.

"I don't really think it's *all* my fault," Anise agreed. "But if I hadn't gone over there in the first place, she wouldn't have gotten upset. She even mentioned the fire and she hasn't said anything about that in years." Anise looked at her hands without thought, running her thumbs over her palms. She shivered as she remembered Bishop kissing her scars.

"What were you discussing right before she knocked over her teacup?"

Anise bit her bottom lip, Madelyn's question bringing her back to the matter at hand. "We were talking about Sarah. Rachel thinks she's in love again. She said something about her 'vanishing into a hole' when that happens. I think she meant that Sarah gets obsessed but she didn't have the right word. Sarah hasn't mentioned anything but then again, she never does."

Madelyn stilled. "That's funny. I suspected she'd met someone new as well. There's definitely something going on."

"Why do you say that?"

"It's just a feeling. She seems more anxious than usual and everything has to be just right."

"She's going nuts over this show, if that's what you're talking about. I'll be so glad when Friday gets here and we can get it behind us."

"That's exactly what I mean. When her personal life starts getting complicated, she wants to control everything else to compensate. No detail is too small to escape her scrutiny and she becomes super critical—it's a typical coping mechanism for people like her. I've seen her do it time and time again. And nothing's more complicated than love, as you and I both know." Madelyn smiled over her half glasses. "I guess that's one thing that's the same no matter who you fall in love with."

That was something she could understand completely. Anise's feelings for Bishop had reached a convoluted pinnacle tonight.

"I suspect you're beginning to feel the same way. Am I right?"

"Is it that obvious?"

Dropping her rag, Madelyn tilted her head. "You're falling in love with Bishop, aren't you?"

"Are you going to fuss at me, too? Sarah hates him."

"I don't care what Sarah thinks. I'm asking *you*."

Anise didn't bother to say yes. "I don't want to feel the way that I do but I can't seem to stop it."

"What's wrong with loving him?"

Anise met her friend's eyes. "You know me better than anyone. I don't have to explain that to you, Madelyn."

"That's true," she said softly, "but maybe you need to explain it to yourself."

Anise stared at her.

"It's time for a gut-check, honey. You like the guy, he likes you. You're both available with no entanglements. There's no good reason for the two of you not to get together. The only thing holding you back is your fear."

"And your point is?"

Anise's lame attempt to get Madelyn off track only made her smile. "No matter Rachel's other problems, she was right about one thing. You can't live your whole life behind a wall, Anise. You've got to come out from behind it sooner or later."

"Something might happen if I do that."

"That's right," Madelyn agreed. "Something *good* might happen. You might have

fun, get married again, become a mother…
Think of the possibilities."

"And what happens if it doesn't work
out?"

"You suffer, then you get over it. It
happens all the time. People survive. You
would, too." She put her hands on Anise's
shoulders and looked her in the eye. "You
aren't eight years old anymore, Anise.
You're thirty-three. When you lost your
mother, you weren't equipped to cope.
Things aren't that way anymore. You're a
grown-up. You would be hurt but it
wouldn't be like it was back then. You have
the skills to handle disappointment now."

Anise blinked and looked down.
Madelyn's voice brought her eyes back up.

"Don't waste your life being scared to
love, Anise. Your mother wouldn't have
wanted that and neither should you."

BISHOP ACCOMMODATED Donna Capanna
to the extent that he could. After questioning her some more, he put her in a holding
cell where she could think about her con-
fession a little bit more.

But he didn't believe her for a minute.

And neither, it turned out, did her attorney.

Too inexperienced to know better, Martin Chamberlain nervously sipped the coffee Bishop had finally gotten for him.

"She called me at home about eight o'clock," he explained, "and insisted I bring her over here." As if remembering his role in the play, he straightened his tie. "But, of course, I can't say any more than that. Client-attorney privilege, you know."

"Where'd she get the weapon?"

"I don't know," he answered readily. "They have a family ranch out in west Texas. Her father's a hunter and she can drop a deer from half a mile away so I guess it makes sense."

"Capanna wasn't shot with a deer rifle," Bishop said.

The attorney shrugged.

"What's her daughter think about this?"

"I doubt she even knows. She and Donna don't really talk that much. It's…kinda tense between them."

"Did Donna really hate Capanna that much? It doesn't seem to me she actually

needed those payments he was behind on."
During the short interview Bishop had con-
ducted, Donna had repeatedly insisted she
was angry at Kenneth for not paying his
child support on time and had wanted to
teach him a lesson.

"Money is always an issue," Chamberlain admitted. "I know it doesn't look that
way, but Donna can spend it like you
wouldn't believe. Her Neiman bills alone
would choke a normal man. Our firm
manages the family accounts so I know."

"What about the alibi? Brittany confirmed
it when I interviewed her, remember? She
said she and her mother had had dinner that
night with her grandparents and they confirmed that. Did Donna tell her what to say?"

The young lawyer pursed his lips. "I
can't discuss that."

"Which means yes."

Chamberlain stayed silent.

"I can see the daughter backing up the
mother, but would Donna's parents have
lied for her?" Bishop's voice grew thoughtful. "They seemed like pretty straight
arrows to me when I talked to them earlier."

"Donna's their only child," the lawyer replied. "You know what it's like… Most folks would do anything to protect their kids, no matter what."

Bishop stared at the clueless young man, then nodded slowly, his words sparking an idea that made this whole mess clear. "You might be right," he said. "More than you even realize."

BISHOP CALLED early the following morning, but he didn't wake Anise. She had been up for hours putting the finishing touches on the last few pieces that would be in the show. When she saw his name on the caller ID, her pulse took an extra beat.

"Thank you," she said when she picked up the phone.

"For what?"

"I had two guardian angels last night," she replied. "I slept pretty well with those cars parked by the curb."

"We're here to serve and protect." He sounded distant.

"Well, I definitely felt protected," she said.

"That's good," he replied, "because

now I'd like to serve you. I'll be there in ten minutes to take you to breakfast. We need to talk."

His voice made it clear there wasn't another option. "Okay," she said cautiously. "I'll be waiting."

Wondering what was up, she slipped out of her shorts and T-shirt and changed into a sundress. It was only nine but the thermometer outside her patio door read ninety-three. By the time she got on her sandals and lipstick, he was ringing the doorbell.

With a look of appreciation that warmed her more than the temperature, he took in her dress, kissed her, then walked her to the car. A few minutes later they pulled into the parking lot of the nearest Denny's.

Stopping at the first booth, they sat down and ordered. Anise didn't have a clue what might be going on until Bishop reached out and took her hand.

"Donna Capanna came into the station last night." His eyes met Anise's over the table. "She claims she killed Kenneth."

A wave of shock rolled over Anise. "Are you kidding me?"

"No. She confessed," he repeated. "But I don't believe her."

Their waitress came and took their order; then Bishop explained his reasoning. By the time she returned with their coffee, Anise could see his point.

"But why would Donna admit to a crime she didn't do?"

"It's not unheard of," he said, emptying a packet of sugar into the steaming mug before him. "But in this case, I think I know why. Her lawyer said something that clicked for me. I could be wrong, but it made me wonder."

"What did he say?"

"We were talking about Donna's parents giving her an alibi for that night. He said most parents would do anything to protect their kid and that's when it sunk in."

Anise took only a second to follow his words. "Brittany…" she breathed. "Oh, my gosh… Do you really think it's possible? Could Donna be covering up for Brittany?"

With a thoughtful expression, Bishop tapped his spoon against the edge of his mug. Watching him, Anise was struck again by how much he cared. None of these individuals had been known to him a month ago, but he was doing his best to solve this case. He was as devoted to his job as she was to hers, but the consequence of his success was a little more significant than getting a bad review. She hadn't thought it possible, but she admired him even more.

"I don't know," he said. "But I sure as hell don't want to make a mistake either way. My initial impression was that the girl didn't have anything to do with it, but now I have to wonder."

"And Robin?"

He shook his head. "Donna insists she didn't have anything to do with her death so I'm assuming that means she believes Brittany had nothing to do with it as well. The two murders have to be linked, though."

"What's next?"

The waitress brought their plates before he could answer. He took a bite of his scrambled eggs then spoke. "I was hoping you could tell me," he said.

Anise's fork stopped in midair. "Me?"

"What do you think?" he asked. "You know all the players."

She shook her head hopelessly. "I'm not a cop, Bishop. I don't know—"

He stopped her. "I don't *want* a cop's opinion," he replied. "I asked *you*. I want to know what you think."

She realized he was serious. Putting her fork down, she wrapped her fingers around her coffee mug and tried to organize her thoughts. Finally, she spoke. "I think you're right. I don't think Brittany or Donna killed Kenneth or Robin. Robin and Kenneth's murders *have* to be connected. It would be too much of a coincidence for them not to be. Which means, Donna would have had to have killed them both and that definitely doesn't make sense."

"Go on."

"The same would have to be said for Brittany. If Donna *is* covering up for her daughter, then *that* means Britt had to have killed them both, too. Which is even less logical. She hardly knew Robin and even if she did, I don't see Brittany being sophisticated enough to pull off a fake suicide and her father's murder. She's only a teenager. An angry one, yes, but still, just a teenager. I know her better than you do and I can say that for sure. In addition, that explanation wouldn't account for the missing funds."

"Exactly. So, if Donna and Brittany are eliminated as suspects, who's left?"

"Robin," Anise said. "She must have killed Kenneth then committed suicide."

Anise listened carefully as Bishop told her about the ballistics reports. The same gun had been used on Robin *and* Kenneth.

"You knew this all along. But you don't trust the conclusion...or you wouldn't have asked me what I thought."

He smiled. "You understand me too well."

"Then where does that leave you?"

His expression turned more serious. "More confused than ever," he replied, "because Sarah told me Robin was with her, remember?"

"I do," Anise said. "I was at the gallery before I met Kenneth for dinner and Sarah said she and Robin were going out that evening. Then after Kenneth was shot, they showed up together."

"Would Sarah have lied to protect Robin?"

"I don't see why. They'd broken up already and even if they had still been together, I don't think Sarah would protect her."

"Did you say anything yet to Sarah about the money?"

"No." Anise pulled in her bottom lip. "I haven't found the right time." She paused. "So what's going to happen to Donna?"

"I'm not sure. I released her but she complained to everyone who would listen. Apparently legal procedures, like warrants and proof, don't mean much to her. She wanted me to leave her in jail. Period. At the very least I have to have some suspicion that she was telling the truth and I don't. The D.A. would laugh me out of her office if I bothered her with this. Besides, who knows? What if Donna changed her mind? Then I'd get hit with an illegal arrest suit. It was definitely a no-win situation."

They talked more as they finished their

breakfast but nothing else came to the surface. They drove home an hour later, Bishop walking Anise to her front door, the hot morning sun throwing their shadows against the house. They paused on the porch.

"I wish I could have helped more." Anise looked up at Bishop. The line of his jaw was tight and she wanted to run her fingers down it. She kept her hands at her side but that took a lot of effort.

"You did help," he answered. "But I'm getting frustrated with this case. It's taking turns I don't like." He glanced behind her, his eyes skipping over the windows along her living room. She'd closed all her blinds last night when she'd come back from Madelyn's. "You haven't had any more visitors, have you?"

"Not that I'm aware of," she replied.

"That's good." He lifted his hand to her face and stroked her cheek, just as she'd imagined doing to him a second before. "Are you ready for the show tomorrow night?"

Distracted by his caress, it took a second for her to understand. "At the gallery?"

"Is there another one?" He grinned.

She tried to cover up. "No, no, that's the only one. And yes, I think I'm ready. I have a few more things to take care of but the boxes are almost all finished." She realized then that she hadn't actually asked him to come. "You are going to be there, aren't you?"

"I wouldn't miss it for the world," he said. "I'll come get you early and we can have dinner first."

She couldn't help it; her face fell.

"No?" he said.

"I can't. I promised Sarah I'd be there an hour before. If I don't show up, she'll have a fit."

"That's okay," he replied. "I'll take you home when it's over. That could be even better...."

Anise lifted her eyes to his, her heart doing a joyful dance, Madelyn's advice coming back to her in a rush. "I think I'd like that," she said slowly. "Let's count on it."

CHAPTER FIFTEEN

THE FOLLOWING DAY, Bishop left the office early. For some reason, I10 was clear and he sailed home where Blanco was ecstatic to see him. The case looped through his mind without stopping but some of the worry fell from his shoulders as he took the dog for a run in the park two blocks from his house. They came back an hour later and Bishop couldn't tell who stank more—him or the animal. He hosed down the Lab and fed him, then stepped into the shower himself. By six he was dressed and ready to go. Anise's show didn't open for another hour but since they weren't going out, Bishop decided to stroll the downtown block where Kenneth Capanna had been shot one more time. He'd had Carter canvass the area twice and Bishop had followed up as well. No one had seen anything but going back to the scene after this much time had passed meant he would view everything through a different set of eyes. If he was lucky, he'd catch something new.

He parked the Crown Vic just outside the gallery and wondered if Anise was there. He thought about going inside to see but he didn't. The more room he gave her, the better she responded. She reminded him of a cat he'd had as a kid. If he ignored it, the animal would seek him out and rub against his legs to purr in quiet contentment. If he sought out the creature, it'd run the other way. To hell with his job. He wanted her to come to him tonight so he was determined to play it cool.

Walking down the street toward the restaurant, just as he had a few days after the shooting, Bishop patted his pocket, the six-pack of photos he'd had made just in case stiff against his shirt.

At the corner, he turned south. This side of the block was lined with offices and shops, the sidewalks crowded with people leaving their jobs and heading for the parking garages nearby or the bus stop one street over. When he headed north, things changed drastically. There was very little foot traffic. An abandoned garage filled one side of the street and only a couple of seedy bars sat on the other side.

He stared at the glass-fronted businesses. He'd been in both several times, asking questions but getting nothing. He started to turn but a reflection caught his eye. A bum, pushing the ubiquitous shopping cart, three dogs tied to the side of it, was making his way into the garage. Bishop increased his pace and caught up with the guy just before he vanished into the shadows.

"Hey, buddy. Can you talk to me for a minute?"

The man turned to eye Bishop, his gaze sharp. He wasn't as old as Bishop had guessed, but that wasn't too surprising. Life on the street wasn't easy. "Whaddaya want?"

"Just some info," Bishop said. "You stay around here?"

"It's my corner," the guy said defensively. "You wanna spot here, you're going have to deal with Butch." He nodded toward the largest dog tied to the handle of the shopping cart. Butch looked to be about fifteen years old and was missing half his front teeth. He obliged his master, though, and growled convincingly.

Bishop held up his hands. "No, no. I'm not interested in that. The corner's all yours. I just want to ask you some questions. I'm taking a survey. I came through here about a month ago but I didn't see you."

"I was on vacation," the man cackled. "Went down to Miami for a couple weeks, but the damn storms kept coming in so I took a bus back here."

"There was a murder around the corner. A shooting. I was wondering if you might have seen anything."

He stared at Bishop with suspicious eyes. "Survey, my ass. You're a cop, ain't cha?"

Bishop didn't bother to lie. He peeled a twenty off his money clip and held it out. "My money's still green."

The bum snatched the bill and it disappeared into his pocket.

"You gonna give me anything for that?" Bishop asked.

"What do you want?"

"Did you see anyone that night?" Bishop asked patiently. "Anyone unusual?"

"You mean not homeless?"

"I mean someone unusual. Someone you don't normally see."

"Maybe."

Bishop looked at him, then handed over another twenty.

"There might have been somebody," he said. "Run by with a sweatshirt thingie on. Looked warm," he added with a note of envy.

Bishop stiffened. He was the first person to confirm what the parking attendant saw. "Did it have a hood on it?"

"Don't remember."

"Was it gray?"

"Everything's gray down here."

Bishop pulled out the six-pack. He'd slipped three cops' photos into the slots, Donna Capanna's, Brittany Capanna's, and the picture he'd taken from Robin Estes's apartment of her and Sarah Levy. He didn't expect anything but he held it out to the bum anyway.

He tilted it to catch the remaining sunlight, then chewed on his bottom lip. "Coulda been," he said almost to himself. "But not for sure…"

"Which one?" Bishop demanded.

The guy lifted a grimy finger and tapped it against the photo of Robin.

"She stopped on the corner and looked back," he said, "and that's when I noticed 'er." His eyes came up to Bishop's. "She did have on a hood," he said as if suddenly remembering. "And it was gray."

"Are you sure it was this woman?" Bishop pointed to Robin. "Did you get a good look?"

"Not 'er," the bum said with irritation. "It was the other one—the dark-haired one."

Bishop blinked in confusion. He pointed again, this time to Sarah. "This is the woman you saw?"

"That's 'er," the bum said. "Now getta outta my way. I got things to do and places to go."

BISHOP WAS LATE.

Anise tried to keep from staring at the door but every time the bell sounded, she found herself turning to see who was entering the gallery. Finally, pulling her into a corner wearing a fake smile, Sarah held her by the arm, snagged a glass of champagne from a passing waiter and thrust it at her.

"What is wrong with you?" She waved at someone across the room and made a five-minute motion with her hand. "You need to focus, Anise. I saw Harvé Betecl trying to talk to you and you practically ignored the man. Do you know who he is?"

"He's an art dealer from Los Angeles," Anise answered with distraction. "I talked to him."

"But not with any enthusiasm."

She gave Sarah an exasperated look. "He's a bore and he has bad breath."

"That's true," Sarah conceded, "but he's a bore with bad breath who has access to the kind of clients we want interested in you. You could have paid a little more attention to him. Suck up a little."

"You're my agent," Anise replied. "*You*

suck up to him. I'm looking for Bishop. He should have been here by now."

The skin over Sarah's jaw went taut, the spotlights overhead making her cheeks look like two blades. "This is business, Anise. Get your head straight. Forget about that damned man and concentrate on your work."

Sarah's voice was so cutting, Anise took a step back. Sarah tightened her fingers and stopped her.

"I'm sorry," she said quickly. "I shouldn't have spoken that way. It's just that this show is so important. And you've worked so hard for it. I want it to be everything that it can be."

Anise stared at her friend as she shook off her touch, a confused set of emotions rising inside her, anger beating the others to the top. "Then maybe you should bring out the piece I made for Bishop that you purchased the other night. Several people have asked me about it. If you want a good sale, where is it?"

Sarah's gaze slid away from Anise's to someone behind her. She dipped her head toward them. "We need to talk about that."

"There's nothing to discuss," Anise said.

"They announced at the HPD Children's Charity gala that you were going to resell it here. Some of the same people are here tonight and they want to see it."

"I changed my mind."

"You what?" Anise stared in surprise.

"I decided not to show it," she said. "It's not representative of your style. I don't want it floating around since you're not going to pursue that avenue."

Anise's suspicions rushed over her in a flood. Now she understood Sarah's motivation for buying the piece in the first place. "What makes you think that? I enjoyed working on it. I may very well—"

"You can't go around making boxes that look like they belong in nurseries, Anise. That's not your way and it never will be. Your art is dark, remember? It has a pathos, an angst, that you have to continue."

"I can't believe you're doing this—"

"We'll talk about it after the show." Sarah stepped around Anise but Anise reached out to stop her this time.

"I want to talk about it now."

"Now isn't the time." Sarah's eyes flared. "We'll talk about it later—"

"Talk about what later?"

Anise drew a sharp breath, Bishop's tall form materializing between the two women. If he'd heard more of the conversation or sensed the tension, his expression didn't reveal it.

Sarah took her chance and fled without another word. Anise glared at her retreating back and tried to regain her composure.

"Are you okay?"

Anise looked up. He *had* heard and he *had* sensed.

"No," she said tightly. "I'm *not* okay." She explained the situation, her fingers gripping her champagne glass so tightly she was surprised the stem didn't snap in two.

Bishop listened, then put his arm around her shoulder and bent down to kiss her. His touch was enough to calm her, her anger seeping away before he began to speak.

"Blow it off," he said. "She's playing with your head. Don't let it get to you."

"But why would she do that?"

"I don't know." His answer came easily

enough but his expression told her there was more. "Let it rest for right now. Talk about it tomorrow," he suggested. "You can sell that box a thousand times over so you aren't missing out on anything if she doesn't show it tonight."

Anise wanted to argue with him but she let the matter drop. Bishop was right.

And somehow, even if he wasn't, it didn't seem important anymore.

He was there and that's all that counted.

WITHOUT BEING OBVIOUS about it, Bishop trailed Sarah Levy as she talked to her guests. They ranged the gamut from obviously wealthy three-piece suit types to a few who looked like they'd be more at home at Joe's Ice House with the other bikers. She greeted them all with an equal amount of interest, however, her praise for Anise's work never-ending. She was pretty amazing, actually. As the evening passed, he found himself impressed. Sarah Levy knew her stuff and even more importantly, she knew how to work her customers. On more than one occasion, he watched her manipulate a lukewarm interest into a four-figure sale. She was good.

But was she also a killer?

Four weeks ago, Bishop would never have given the question a second thought. Sarah was Anise's champion, right? Her biggest fan, her friend for life, her closest ally, but the bum's ID had made him look at the art dealer in a different way.

And watching her tonight had made him conscious of just how great a manipulator she really was.

But why would Sarah even want Kenneth dead? Or Robin, either, for that matter? And what about the money? When he found himself outside the corridor that led to Sarah's office, temptation overcame good sense. He threw a look over his shoulder, then slipped down the hallway.

Her office door was locked. He slipped a credit card out and tried to jimmy the lock but failed.

He cursed under his breath and tried the next door. Considering the layout of the block, he thought the door led to the space adjacent to the gallery but Anise had never mentioned Sarah owning that building as well. To his surprise, his credit card worked this time.

This door opened with a whisper and Bishop found himself inside what seemed to be a warehouse, the unpartitioned space as large as, if not larger, than the gallery out front. He estimated the size then realized he'd been correct. He was standing in the boarded-up building that shared the gallery's western wall.

In the center of the warehouse sat a mock-up of a room.

Complete with doors and windows but without a roof, it looked as though it'd been neatly excised from the side of a home and set down inside the warehouse, the exterior siding made of wood and painted a pale blue. Through the glass of the windows, edged with frilly pink curtains, he could see the outline of some furniture, a bed, a chest, a chair. He shook his head. Weird, he thought. Too weird for words.

He approached it slowly, making his way around the perimeter until he found the door. Opening it, he stepped inside, the thought striking him immediately that the space felt strangely familiar.

But it couldn't be.

The room, clearly decorated to suit a child, was one he'd never seen, much less been inside.

He walked to the bed, jabbed a finger into the mattress, then moved on to the table. It was small and black with a round top. The nearby chest was painted a light ivory color, small butterflies flitting over the top and sides as if they'd momentarily landed for a rest. Everything was full-sized and operational, the top of the chest covered with a few scattered rocks and a small purse made of sequins. The drawers were filled with clothing. He pulled out a shirt and held it up. It was new, size six. For a girl.

Still holding the top, his confusion growing, he turned around. Another door led off the bedroom. He crossed the room and opened it to find a closet, complete with scattered tennis shoes and books on the floor, dresses hanging on the poles. Closing the door behind him, he frowned and tried to make some sense of the situation.

He was still standing there when Sarah Levy opened the door and walked inside.

She didn't seem surprised to see him.

"What are you doing here? That door was supposed to be locked," she asked in a conversational manner. "This space isn't open to the public."

I guess not, he wanted to say. *It's too damned creepy for normal people.*

"I didn't realize you had this building, too."

"I just acquired it. And I'd appreciate it if you didn't mention it to Anise, either."

"Why is that?"

"She thinks I should be more prudent with my business. I like to take risks, though." She tilted her head slightly. "I think it makes life a little more interesting, don't you?"

Just as before, he ignored her question and asked one of his own. "What is it?" he said, pointing toward the room.

"I build sets," she said. "For local theater productions. I'm doing this one for a community group out in Katy. I build them here, then take them apart and reconstruct them on-site. It's cheaper for them and easier for me." She walked to where he stood and took the little girl's shirt from his hands.

"Seems like a lot of work."

"Not really." Stepping to the bed, she laid the T-shirt on the mattress, smoothed it and folded it carefully. Sitting down beside it a second later, her hand resting protectively on it, she stared at him. She seemed comfortable in the room, he realized, as if she'd sat there many times before.

"Have you been working on this long?"

She smiled, clearly sensing his thoughts. "Long enough. I get attached to them."

"It seems familiar to me."

"I can't imagine why." She laughed easily. "Unless you've seen *The Little Girl's Room*. It was produced a few years back off-off-off Broadway."

"I'm afraid I missed it."

She stood up and ran a hand over the bedspread. It matched the curtain, he noticed, as she put the shirt back into the dresser.

"Actually, it's a pretty fascinating little play," she said. "There's a lot of depth to it and the secondary characters are really quite interesting. Unfortunately it's not a story most people would understand…or ever appreciate."

"And why is that?"

She raised her eyes to his, her gaze dark and unreadable. "People are stupid," she said flatly, "and they don't like to be presented with anything different from what they expect. They want fast food, bad TV and boring entertainment. If you give them anything else, they get confused."

"That's a pretty negative view of the world."

"Maybe. But it's the truth. I would think you'd know that better than any of us."

"I deal with criminals," he said lightly. "Maybe they're smarter than the average art critic."

ANISE DESPAIRED of ever being able to leave the gallery but the crowd thinned gradually until there were only a few couples left. Walking through the almost empty space, still unsettled over her spat with Sarah, she'd begun to wonder if Bishop had gone home without her when she spotted him and Sarah coming from the back of the gallery. "Where have you been?" she asked. "I've been looking all over for you. I'm ready to leave."

"We still have some guests," Sarah pointed out.

"I realize that," Anise said. "But I think you can handle them. I'd like to go home. I'm exhausted." Her voice was clipped. Something had shifted in their friendship, it said, and it would take awhile for it to shift back.

"You're upset with me because I didn't bring out the charity box, aren't you?"

"I don't want to talk about it right now."

"C'mon," Sarah said, nudging her with her elbow. "I know what's best for you, Anise. I always have. Do you really think I'd do anything—*anything*—that would jeopardize your career in the tiniest way?"

Anise felt Bishop's stare as it went back and forth between her and Sarah.

"I'm going home," she said tightly. "If you want to discuss it, we'll talk in the morning." Taking Bishop's arm, Anise left the gallery without another look.

They reached her street twenty minutes later, Anise pulling her car into her driveway, Bishop parking his Crown Vic behind her. Walking inside the house, Anise dropped her purse on the nearest chair and reached for the light switch. Bishop's hand stopped her. Then he pulled her into his arms.

"Don't," he whispered. "Leave the lights off."

Anise started to argue, but she'd argued enough for one night, the stress of the evening's hypocrisy overcoming her without any warning. The critics, the buyers, the other artists…all at once, the world she'd been living in seemed false and pretentious, her efforts to box up her emotions just as pointless.

She wanted something *real*.

She lifted her face to Bishop's and kissed him, looping her hand around his neck to draw him to her. A heartbeat later, he wrapped his arms around her, their mutual desire palpable in the confines of the darkened room.

They shed their clothes and their inhibitions. When the sun came up the following morning, nothing was as it had been before.

ANISE WAS NOWHERE in sight when Bishop woke up. For a moment, he wondered if he'd dreamed their whole encounter, but then he realized he was in her bedroom. He sat up in the bed. It had really happened.

They'd made love for hours.

The door opened softly and he turned to watch her. She wore the same robe he'd seen her in the first time he'd come to her house. It was belted loosely and her hair hung in tendrils around her face.

They stared at each other in the filtered light coming through the blinds, then she crossed the space that separated them and perched on the side of the bed. Once again, he got the feeling she might flee if he said the wrong thing, so he said nothing at all. He reached for her instead, and pulled her toward him. They shared a long, deep kiss, then she eased away from him. He read her remorse in her gaze.

"Don't," he said softly.

Her eyes widened.

"Don't regret what we did." He ran his thumb over the ridges on her palm, then raised her hand to his lips. He kissed the scars lightly, his stare never leaving her face. "Throw me out, kiss me again, crawl back into the bed. You make the choice, but don't be unhappy about last night. If anyone's to blame for doing something wrong, it's me. There's no reason for me to be in your bed while I'm trying to solve Kenneth's murder."

"You're going to do the right thing, regardless."

"I know that and you know that…but it wouldn't matter if the press found out. Or my boss."

"I'm not very good at relationships," she said after a moment.

"I told you before, I don't exactly have a sterling record in that department myself."

"I work too much. I don't pay attention. I day-dream. Kenneth told me once that I was a hard person to love."

Bishop eased the back of his hand down the side of her jawline. She turned and kissed his knuckles.

"I think he had that backward," Bishop countered.

She nodded as her hands went to the belt on her robe and she undid the knot. Bishop slipped his fingers under the fabric and pushed it off her shoulders, her halfhearted objections going with it. A second later, she climbed beneath the sheets and they started all over again.

BISHOP LEFT a little while later, reluctantly explaining he had work to do. Anise watched him drive off, an immediate ache rising inside her at his absence. Ignoring her reaction, she went back to the bedroom but the feeling hit her even harder when she saw the twisted sheets. She turned around and went to her studio, her mind tumbling a thousand different directions. Without even realizing what she was doing, she began to sketch, her brain divided between her work and what had just happened with her and Bishop. The last few hours replayed themselves in her head, scenes from the gallery superimposing themselves on images of the two of them in bed, their skin slicked, their limbs tangled. She went from scared to angry to confused. By the time she put down her pencil, several points had sorted themselves out.

Two people didn't connect as she and Bishop had unless something special was going on. She had opened her arms to him last night but he'd slipped into her heart when she hadn't been watching. She hadn't wanted to fall in love with him. It was happening, though, and she didn't know how to stop it.

She only wished Sarah could be happy for her.

Anise had always felt as if she and Sarah totally understood each other but after last night she wasn't sure that was still the case. Sarah had made a big mistake in refusing to show Bishop's box but she'd made an even bigger one in her opinion of the man himself.

Either way, it didn't really matter.

The connection Bishop and Anise had

made couldn't be permanent. Because no matter how much sense Madelyn and Rachel had made when they'd talked to Anise about real love, neither of them appreciated Anise's situation. She couldn't afford to love Bishop the way he deserved. Love like that, total and complete, always ended up with someone hurt and she couldn't handle that kind of pain.

She stopped midafternoon to grab something to eat, then continued to find solace in the rhythm of her work. When her grandfather clock struck midnight, she glanced up from her sketch pad. That's when she saw the blinking light on the telephone. Anise picked up her messages and let them play over the speaker.

Sarah had called dozens of times, her voice sounding strained as it echoed in the darkened studio.

"Anise, I want to talk about the show. Give me a ring."

"Anise, where are you? This is the third time I've called...."

"Are you there and not picking up because you're mad at me?"

"*I just want to talk, okay? I'm sorry if I upset you.*"

"*Please call me, Anise. I really need to talk to you. Okay? Please?*"

CHAPTER SIXTEEN

BISHOP WENT STRAIGHT into the office, his mind filled with images of Anise and all he needed to do. He'd put a call in to Donna Capanna's parents to push them a bit. He knew Donna was innocent but he wanted to be able to prove it, the irony making him shake his head. He wanted to go over the statements again, too, especially Sarah's, to see how they jibed with the bum's ID of her photo. In the end, to pin Capanna's murder on her, he would have to have more than a homeless man's word that he'd seen Sarah Levy running by. The set Bishop had found in the back of the gallery continued to bug him, too. Why had it felt so familiar? He should have asked Anise about it but they'd had a few other things on their minds. After he finished with the reports, he intended to go to the gallery again. He had a feeling the answer to his questions could be found there.

Grabbing a cup of coffee, he headed to his desk, juggling the cup, his briefcase and his thoughts on the woman he'd held in his arms all night long. Their time together had made him realize the depth of his feelings and facing them head-on, he found himself confused. She had let herself come out from behind the wall but would it be a permanent situation? Things were too comfortable for her behind it. She wouldn't relinquish that to take a chance on him but he was willing to risk his career for her. What chance would they have?

Everything disappeared from his mind when he rounded the corner and saw who was sitting in his chair.

Brittany Capanna jumped to her feet.

He recovered as quickly as he could. "Whoa, you scared me," Bishop teased. "I thought I'd been replaced there for a minute."

She looked at him with an uncertain expression, then seemed to realize he was joking. A tentative smile came before it fled, her tone serious. "I need to talk to you."

"Talk away." He set his load down on the desk.

"It's about my mom."

Bishop sat down behind his desk and the teenager took the chair on the other side.

"She didn't kill my dad." The smart-aleck, half-wit attitude was gone. Brittany was tuned in, her words blunt.

"Then who did?"

"I don't know," the girl said earnestly. "But it wasn't my mom. She was with her boyfriend that night. He's a married guy in our neighborhood. He probably won't talk to you because he doesn't want his wife to know he's been fooling around but I know she was with him."

"Okay…" Bishop drew the word out, the teenager's revelation soaking in.

"His name is Alan Herrington," she offered. "And he lives at 1634 Spring Shadows." She dug into the pocket of her jeans then pushed a scrap of paper toward Bishop. "That's his cell phone number. I got it off Mom's phone."

"So your grandparents lied?"

"Yeah. She asked them to and they said they would."

"Why do you think your mother confessed?"

She sat quietly for a second or two, then she answered him, her eyes on the carpet. "She thinks I did it. She read those e-mails and my diary. Then she tried to figure out where I was that night and she couldn't because I lied to her about where I was. She decided then that I killed him." She lifted her eyes to Bishop's. "But I didn't and I can prove that, too."

"How?"

"I told her I went to Vicki's house—Vicki's this dumb girl down the street that my mom likes—but I really went to a rave out in Kingwood. There were a lot of kids there. I don't know if they'll back me up, but that's where I was, I swear."

"How old are you, Brittany?"

She seemed surprised by his question. "Sixteen."

"Those raves can get pretty rough. Especially for a girl your age."

Her chin jutted out in self-defense, then fell. "I know that. I realized it after I got there. I don't think I'll be doing that again."

"What about your visits to Anise? You seem pretty angry at her."

Her voice slipped up an octave, her emotions barely under control. "I still am. She stole my dad from us and probably took all his money, too. But that hasn't got anything to do with this. My mom didn't kill him and I wanted to make sure you knew that."

Leaning back in his chair, Bishop considered her words in silence. "Why are you telling me this now, Brittany? You had other opportunities. Why wait?"

"I didn't think my mom would go this far. I—I didn't understand that she…"

"Loved you that much?"

She looked up at him, her face tight with fear. "We fight all the time and I thought… I don't know. I just didn't believe she'd do something like this. Dolores knew Mom and I were both lying and she told me I had to do the right thing or I'd never forgive myself."

"Who's Dolores?"

"You met her," Brittany said. "She's our maid. She brought me here. She's waiting downstairs."

Somehow Bishop wasn't surprised. "You're close to her?"

"She's worked for us for a long time. Even before Dad left. I can, you know, talk to her sometimes."

Because she was the only adult in Brittany's life who took the time to listen.

Rising to her feet, the teenager reached into the other pocket of her jeans and took out another crumpled piece of paper. "This is a list of kids I saw at the rave," she said. "And their phone numbers. If you could talk to them without their parents knowing, it'd be better. I don't wanna get them in trouble."

Bishop stood up, too. "Thank you."

She mumbled "You're welcome," then paused, her face screwed into an expression that told him she was holding back tears. "Do you think you'll get him?" she asked, her voice thick. "You know, the guy who killed my dad?"

"I'm trying my best."

He watched the young girl leave, his

thoughts going full circle. A moment later, grabbing his notebook and jacket, he was downstairs and out on the sidewalk.

THE LIGHTS WERE OFF inside the gallery, the door locked securely. He banged on the glass anyway, then turned down the block and came back up the alley. A red Jeep was parked on an angle next to the loading dock that went to the building next door. He made his way toward the stairs going up to the back door, then pushed his way inside without bothering to knock.

The scent of gasoline was overpowering. He scanned the empty warehouse. Sarah was nowhere in sight as he strode toward the set he'd examined the night before. His jaw going tight, he stepped inside the open doorway and studied the space again, the images falling in place with a force that stole his breath. He'd returned to Anise's studio last night, this time with her permission. Looking at her projects, he'd come across the box he'd picked up the first time he'd been there. She had waited beside him, then answered his unspoken question.

"It represents my childhood bedroom," she'd explained.

"Where you were trapped when the fire broke out?"

"Yes." She moved the sequin over with her fingernail. "I always loved shiny things when I was a kid. Shiny things and books. I was either drawing or reading all the time."

"No dolls for you?"

She'd laughed. "Nope. I wasn't interested in them. Thank God my mother understood. She encouraged my art. She even let me paint my furniture. I don't think there's too many moms around who would go that far...."

It hadn't made sense then, but standing in Sarah's set and replaying Anise's words everything came together. He closed his eyes, an unwelcome realization setting in.

Sarah hadn't built a set. She'd recreated the scene of her greatest accomplishment. Saving Anise. The similarities between the shadow box in Anise's studio and the very place where he stood couldn't be coincidental. The painted chest and table, the sequined purse, the books on the closet floor… Anise had used her artist's license when designing the shadow box but not that much. He recognized the room. His hand went to his cell phone.

Punching out Anise's number, he heard a whisper of sound behind him. He turned but he wasn't fast enough. A wooden two-by-four connected with his head, knocking him to the floor.

ANISE LET HERSELF into the darkened gallery, calling Sarah's name as she opened the door. "Sarah? Are you here? It's me…"

A door closed and Sarah called out. "I'm back here! In the office."

Anise crossed the display area and headed down the corridor, going straight to Sarah's office. The other woman stood. "You're here! I'm so glad you got my messages and came! I was worried about you."

Anise dropped her purse on the chair in front of the desk. She'd been rehearsing what she wanted to say on the way over but all her preparations went out the window when she saw Sarah who still wore the suit she'd had on at the show. She looked a mess, her hair flying around her face, her makeup smudged. Anise stared at her friend in confusion.

"What's going on, Sarah? Is something wrong? You look like you haven't even been home."

Sarah stiffened instantly. "I started working and I guess I lost track of time. Just like you do."

Anise's suspicions increased. Something wasn't right. "You worked all night? But you called me practically every hour, Sarah. Are you...okay?"

"I was concerned about you," she said, her voice rising defensively. "If you'd answered your telephone, then I wouldn't have had to leave so many messages."

"I was busy."

"Doing what?"

"Having a life," Anise said with exasperation. "But that's not what I want to talk about—"

"Were you with Bishop? I saw him kiss you last night."

"It doesn't matter."

"It matters to me."

"Sarah, please… Bishop doesn't have anything to do with this."

"He has everything to do with it. Just like Kenneth did. And Robin, too! They don't know what's right for you. Not like I do. I'm the only one who really cares, Anise. I'm the only one!"

"C'mon, Sarah. Slow down here. I think you're overreacting."

"What about the money, Anise? Is it overreacting to be upset about them stealing from you?"

Anise froze. "You knew what Kenneth and Robin were doing?"

"Of course I knew. I know everything that goes on in your life. But it wasn't Kenneth. Robin was the one doing all the stealing. She'd been taking your money for years. When Kenneth caught her, she killed him. She was a good shot. She took me out to the range the day before and showed me." Sarah shuddered dramatically. "And the day after that, she killed herself. She deserved what she got. She was stealing from you, Anise. That's not right!"

Anise could feel her pulse throbbing in

her neck, her mouth going dry. "You need to calm down, Sarah."

Sarah came to where Anise stood. "I've been calm for years and it's gotten me nowhere. I'm changing my tactics."

"What are you talking about?"

"I'm talking about us," she answered. "You and me. All I've ever wanted for you was the best but all these other people kept getting in the way. They were out to hurt you and I couldn't let that happen. I love you and I know you've always loved me, too. Why wouldn't you?" Her eyes glittered. "I'm the one who saved you from the fire."

"What's that got to do with—" Anise broke off abruptly, her nostrils flaring. She took a step toward the door then stopped. Whirling suddenly, she look back at Sarah. "Do you smell something?" Sarah didn't answer and Anise grabbed her arms, panic rippling through her. "I smell smoke," she cried. "Where's it coming from?"

"You're imagining things, Anise. Please—"

"I'm not imagining anything! There's

something on fire! Call the fire department. I can smell it!" Her eyes began to water. Gray smoke was curling from underneath the door to Sarah's office like a deadly snake. *"Look!"*

Sarah stepped in front of her protectively. "It's okay," she said in her strange, calm voice. "It's all right, Anise. I'm here!"

"We've got to leave!" Anise gripped Sarah's hand so hard the other woman winced. "C'mon! Hurry!"

"Stay calm." Sarah ordered. "We have to decide which way to go. Let me open the door first."

Panic ripped through Anise's chest. She couldn't breathe. She started to push past Sarah but Sarah yanked her back. "No, Anise! It's not safe. Stay behind me."

Holding Anise's hand, Sarah grabbed the jacket she always had hanging by the door and handed it to her. "Put this over your head!"

Anise complied then Sarah threw open the office door. They were instantly overcome by a thick, oily cloud. If Sarah hadn't been with her, Anise would have collapsed with fear, her memories enough to paralyze her.

They fought their way down the dim corridor to the exit in the back. Anise was completely disoriented, then she realized Sarah had taken her into the building next door. Her eyes widened as the sight before her registered. Flames were shooting from the center of the room toward the rafters, a pile of burning lumber fueling their ascent. Something cracked and Anise caught a glimpse of a window as it shattered, shards shooting out in every direction. She ducked but a piece of jagged glass sliced into her cheek, barely missing her eye. She cried out and stumbled, going down to her knees. A red patch on the floor caught her eye, then Sarah jerked her up and they kept going. They made it to the loading dock just as something inside exploded. The rumbling eruption sounded like thunder but it didn't stop. Running down the steps, her hand still holding Anise's, Sarah looked back.

"It's the paint cans I keep in the back," she cried. "They're exploding." As she spoke, an aluminum lid sailed out of the inferno. It whistled an inch above their heads, then hit the building across from them.

They reached the other side of the alley as sirens screamed in the distance. Someone must have called the fire trucks, Anise thought in a daze. The sounds of the wailing sirens drew closer and all at once, struck by their terrifying approach, her mind sharpened and she realized what she'd seen when she stumbled.

It'd been a cell phone. With a red plastic cover on it that was melting because of the heat.

CHAPTER SEVENTEEN

His eyes were open but he couldn't see. Bishop moaned and raised a hand to his temple, his eyes stinging as the warehouse filled with smoke, the crackling sound of burning wood mixing with the noxious smell of paint. Pain ricocheted down his arm at the movement. He had to get out, he told himself. If the flames didn't get him, the smoke would.

Rolling to his side, he propped himself up on one elbow and forced himself onto his knees. Swaying back and forth like a drunken dog, he took a second to gain his bearings, but nothing made any sense. He had no idea where he was. All he knew was who had hit him.

Sarah Levy's rubber-soled shoes had

been the last thing he'd seen before he'd passed out.

He crawled a foot, maybe two, his progress hindered by rib-breaking coughs. He couldn't catch his breath in the blistering heat. His mind filled with the image of Anise's face from the night before, then he collapsed again.

ANISE GRABBED Sarah's arm, the unthinkable becoming the possible. "What have you done?" she cried. "Did you…did you set that fire? Is Bishop in there?"

"He was getting in the way," she said calmly. "After you visited my mother, I realized how serious things were becoming. I saw you that night. I had to protect you."

"That was you at my window? My God, Sarah…"

Sarah continued as though she hadn't heard the question. "I can't have anyone come between the two of us, Anise. Kenneth, Robin, your mom… They didn't understand so I had to take care of them. Nothing can come between us. Surely you see that?"

Anise felt her mouth fall open as she stared at Sarah with disbelief. It seemed as though the words were coming from a long way away, Sarah's mouth moving out of sync with the sounds she was producing. They made no sense, then with a sickening realization, Anise decided they did make sense, a terrible, tragic, unacceptable kind of sense.

She started back toward the burning warehouse but Sarah caught up with her. Pulling her to a stop just as one of the walls collapsed, a cloud of sparks and flames shooting toward the sky, the smell of smoke filling the alley.

"Wait!" Sarah screamed. "You can't go in there, Anise."

"I'm not going to let him die."

"I'll take care of you." Sarah yanked on Anise's arm again. "I did it before, remember? It'll be just like it was then. I took care of things then, I can do it again."

"It's over, Sarah. I'm going in there and you can't stop me." Anise wrenched herself away from the other woman and ran toward the flames. A moment later, Sarah followed.

BISHOP WOKE UP to a hallucination. He thought Anise was beside him, tugging his arm and screaming for him to stand. The fire was still raging, the flames now crawling up the sides of the warehouse, smoke billowing in every direction.

Then he realized he wasn't dreaming.

"Get up!" Anise had both her arms under his and she was trying to lift him. "Get up, Bishop! You have to walk. I can't carry you!"

His mind blurred and he shook his head, a big mistake. "No, no," he muttered. "Lie down with me. Right here. It'll be okay…."

Across the room, something crashed. He narrowed his gaze. His eyes were stinging, but he made out a burning figure wavering in the distance. Trapped between the wall and the door, it stood alone, still and accepting. A bank of flames rose between them and all he could see was fire. Anise screamed, then another boom rattled the building. It sounded like a beam plummeting to the concrete floor, Bishop thought calmly. The roof was caving in. On the other side of the room, the lone figure turned into a column of flame. She didn't call out or scream. She simply stood there.

He shut his eyes. When he opened them again, he was in the hospital.

"SHE REALLY LOVED YOU."

Anise looked up from her sketchbook as Bishop spoke. Sitting in a chair in the corner of her studio, he held a book in his lap but he wasn't reading. "You know that, don't you?"

She put her pencil down. "You're supposed to be recuperating. Not talking."

"We have to talk about it sooner or later. You can't bury something like this and act like it never happened."

"I can."

"Well, you shouldn't."

Anise stood and crossed the room to perch on the footstool before him. Lying on the floor beside Bishop, hoping for a treat, Blanco lifted his head. He and Anise had bonded over the past week while Bishop had recovered at her house. She'd never had a dog before but now she understood the appeal. Total acceptance and absolute love…all on four legs. She reached down and ruffled his head, his yellow fur warm from the patch of sun coming through the window. "I probably do a lot of things I shouldn't." She smiled. "But that's life…."

Bishop took her fingers. "Sarah killed your mother," he said quietly. "There was evil there from a long way back."

Grief, for her friend, for her mother, for the past, rose like a black tide, swamping Anise. She didn't want to accept what had happened. "There was good, too."

He stared at her, his eyes wide under the bandage that covered his temple. "You can say that, knowing what you do?"

"It's the truth." She laced her fingers with his and looked up. "Sarah was a complicated person, Bishop. She wasn't all good and she wasn't all bad. No one is. I hate what she did. My God, you almost died! She killed Kenneth and my mother. Robin, too. But I can't throw out all the years of friendship that we had. She *did* love me and I loved her, too."

"She never wanted you as a lover."

"No." Anise looked out the window. "It

wasn't that kind of relationship. Ever. She didn't see it that way and I never did, either. She just felt she knew what was best for me and she wanted me close to her with no one else between us. Her issue wasn't sexual. If I had to label it, I guess I'd call it a control problem. Though that sounds too simplistic." She and Madelyn had discussed what had happened one day while Bishop had rested. Anise wasn't sure she'd ever understand even though Madelyn had tried her best.

The issues were too complex and the truth had died with Sarah.

Cody Carter had searched her home while Bishop was still in the hospital, though, and he'd found enough to prove her guilt. Sarah's computer, her e-mails to Robin, even her childhood journal… The details had been outlined in her own bold script.

"She wanted what she thought was the best for me and that included a divorce from Kenneth. When I told her I wasn't sure he was going to sign the papers that night, she decided to get rid of him for me." Anise's voice was steady. "He didn't want a divorce because he knew I would take my accounts away from him after the papers were signed."

"But she had to have an alibi…."

Anise nodded. "And that's where Robin came in."

"She and Kenneth were in it together, but she made a big mistake when she told Sarah what they'd done," Bishop mused. "Sarah couldn't let that continue so she blackmailed Robin into giving her an alibi. After that, Sarah had to get rid of Robin."

"Setting her up for Kenneth's murder would have been nothing for Sarah. She had Robin twisted around her finger. The drug comments, the 'self-medicating' thing…Sarah had us all believing Robin was a different person."

"Robin's suicide was supposed to tidy up all the loose ends."

"But it didn't."

"Not after I talked to the bum."

"And the gun?"

"Carter found out yesterday it'd been stolen and used in a robbery three weeks before. Whoever had it must have ditched it. It was too hot. Sarah must have bought it on the street and used it on Kenneth before she gave it to Robin. There *was* residue on her fingers, just like Sarah said. And we have witnesses that put them both at the shooting range. I don't know how she did it but she either convinced Robin to kill herself or she shot her herself. There were no drugs in Robin's system, though."

"Do you think Robin was trying to warn me the night she came to the house?"

"That would be my best guess," he said. "Robin was as much a pawn in Sarah's plans as anyone. Sarah might have sent her to make her look even more crazy, though. It all started unraveling at that point."

"Because of you."

Bishop met her gaze. "Because of *us*. When Sarah saw you and me getting closer, she thought she was going to lose you. Kenneth didn't threaten her like I did because you didn't love him. But when she saw our relationship growing she knew something more was going on. Which meant she couldn't have you to herself any more."

Anise nodded without speaking, a part

of her so numb she couldn't begin to face all the possibilities. If Bishop had died in the fire as Sarah had planned, Anise wasn't sure she could have continued. He'd brought a light into her life she never expected to have. The change in her art had been her first clue but she hadn't realized it then.

He squeezed her hand in sympathy. "Sarah was a master manipulator, Anise. Her parents must have known that from the very beginning. Why else would they have turned the gallery over to her when she was still so young? She forced them to. And they have to have known she set the first fire, too."

Anise had gone to Rachel's assisted living facility to tell her of Sarah's death. Rachel hadn't seemed surprised. In fact, if anything, her face had registered relief mixed with grief.

"Her mother suspected it, I'm sure. I think she tried to warn me about that when I visited, but she couldn't come right out and accuse her daughter of murder. Look what Donna did for Brittany. Parents are going to protect their kids, no matter what. That's how love works. It's too powerful to ignore."

"Is that why you came back for me?"

She looked down at their hands. Their fingers were entwined, hers scarred, his bandaged. "I couldn't let you die in there, Bishop. If that's what love is, then that must be what I feel."

He drew her to him and wrapped his arms around her. "Frankly, after we slept together I wondered if we could make it as a couple. I was willing to risk everything…my career, the case, you name it…for you but I didn't think you were willing to come out from behind your wall and take a chance on me." He pulled back and looked down at her. "Then you saved my life…by risking yours. That's the very definition of love to me. What do you think?"

Her throat went tight. "Love is a scary word for me, Bishop. I…I'm not sure I can manage it just yet."

"Well, I can. I *do* love you, Anise. And I always will."

He kissed her deeply, their mouths meeting, and an emotion that frightened her as much as it pleased her rushed through her. She tightened her grip, her arms around his shoulders, her breasts pushing into his chest. Her lips told him what she couldn't bring herself to say. When he finally lifted his head, their eyes met again and he smiled.

"They're only words," he murmured. "I don't need to hear them as long as I've got you."

Anise held on tightly. "You've got me," she promised, "for as long as you want… and then some."

* * * * *

Mediterranean Nights

Join the guests and crew of
Alexandra's Dream, *the newest luxury ship
to set sail on the romantic Mediterranean,
as they experience
the glamorous world of cruising.*

*A new Harlequin continuity series
begins in June 2007 with
FROM RUSSIA, WITH LOVE
by Ingrid Weaver*

*Marina Artamova books a cabin on the
luxurious cruise ship* Alexandra's
Dream, *when she finds out that her
orphaned nephew and his adoptive
father are aboard. She's determined to
be reunited with the boy...but the
romantic ambience of the ship and her
undeniable attraction to a man
she considers her enemy are about to
interfere with her quest!*

Turn the page for a sneak preview!

Piraeus, Greece

"THERE SHE IS, Stefan. *Alexandra's Dream.*" David Anderson squatted beside his new son and pointed at the dark blue hull that towered above the pier. The cruise ship was a majestic sight, twelve decks high and as long as a city block. A circle of silver and gold stars, the logo of the Liberty Cruise Line, gleamed from the swept-back smokestack. Like some legendary sea creature born for the water, the ship emanated power from every sleek curve—even at rest it held the promise of motion. "That's going to be our home for the next ten days."

The child beside him remained silent, his cheeks working in and out as he sucked furiously on his thumb. Hair so blond it appeared white ruffled against his forehead in the harbor breeze. The baby-sweet scent unique to the very young mingled with the tang of the sea.

"Ship," David said. "Uh, *parakhod*."

From beneath his bangs, Stefan looked at the *Alexandra's Dream*. Although he didn't release his thumb, the corners of his mouth tightened with the beginning of a smile.

David grinned. That was Stefan's first smile this afternoon, one of only two since they had left the orphanage yesterday. It was probably because of the boat—according to the orphanage staff, the boy loved boats, which was the main reason David had decided to book this cruise. Then again, there was a strong possibility the smile could have been a reaction to David's attempt at pocket-dictionary Russian. Whatever the cause, it was a good start.

The liaison from the adoption agency had claimed that Stefan had been taught some English, but David had yet to see evidence of it. David continued to speak, positive his son would understand his tone even if he couldn't grasp the words. "This is her maiden voyage. Her first trip, just like this is our first trip, and that makes it special." He motioned toward the stage that had been set up on the pier beneath the ship's bow. "That's why everyone's celebrating."

The ship's official christening ceremony had been held the day before and had been a closed affair, with only the cruise-line executives and VIP guests invited, but the stage hadn't yet been disassembled. Banners bearing the blue and white of the Greek flag of the ship's owner, as well as the Liberty circle of stars logo, draped the edges of the platform. In the center, a group of musicians and a dance troupe dressed in traditional white folk costumes performed for the benefit of the *Alexandra's Dream*'s first passengers. Their audience was in a festive mood, snapping their fingers in time to the music while the dancers twirled and wove through their steps.

David bobbed his head to the rhythm of the mandolins. They were playing a folk tune that seemed vaguely familiar, possibly from a movie he'd seen. He hummed a few notes. "Catchy melody, isn't it?"

Stefan turned his gaze on David. His eyes were a striking shade of blue, as cool and pale as a winter horizon and far too solemn for a child not yet five. Still, the smile that hovered at the corners of his mouth persisted. He moved his head with the music, mirroring David's motion.

David gave a silent cheer at the interaction. Hopefully, this cruise would provide countless opportunities for more. "Hey, good for you," he said. "Do you like the music?"

The child's eyes sparked. He withdrew his thumb with a pop. *"Moozika!"*

"Music. Right!" David held out his hand. "Come on, let's go closer so we can watch the dancers."

Stefan grasped David's hand quickly, as if he feared it would be withdrawn. In an instant his budding smile was replaced by a look close to panic.

Did he remember the car accident that had killed his parents? It would be a mercy if he didn't. As far as David knew, Stefan had never spoken of it to anyone. Whatever he had seen had made him run so far from the crash that the police hadn't found him until the next day. The event had traumatized him to the extent that he hadn't uttered a word until his fifth week at the orphanage. Even now he seldom talked.

David sat back on his heels and brushed the hair from Stefan's forehead. That solemn, too-old gaze locked with his, and for an instant, David felt as if he looked back in time at an image of himself thirty years ago.

He didn't need to speak the same language to understand exactly how this boy felt. He knew what it meant to be alone and powerless among strangers, trying to be brave and tough but wishing with every fiber of his being for a place to belong, to be safe, and most of all for someone to love him....

He knew in his heart he would be a good parent to Stefan. It was why he had never considered halting the adoption process after Ellie had left him. He hadn't balked when he'd learned of the recent claim by Stefan's spinster aunt, either; the absentee relative had shown up too late for her case to be considered. The adoption was meant to be. He and this child already shared a bond that went deeper than paperwork or legalities.

A seagull screeched overhead, making Stefan start and press closer to David.

"That's my boy," David murmured. He swallowed hard, struck by the simple truth of what he had just said.

That's my *boy*.

"I CAN'T BE PATIENT, RUDOLPH. I'm not going to stand by and watch my nephew get ripped from his country and his roots to live on the other side of the world."

Rudolph hissed out a slow breath. "Marina, I don't like the sound of that. What are you planning?"

"I'm going to talk some sense into this American kidnapper."

"No. Absolutely not. No offence, but diplomacy is not your strong suit."

"Diplomacy be damned. Their ship's due to sail at five o'clock."

"Then you wouldn't have an opportunity

to speak with him even if his lawyer agreed to a meeting."

"I'll have ten days of opportunities, Rudolph, since I plan to be on board that ship."

* * * * *

Follow Marina and David as they join forces to uncover the reason behind little Stefan's unusual silence, and the secret behind the death of his parents....
Look for FROM RUSSIA, WITH LOVE *by Ingrid Weaver in stores June 2007.*

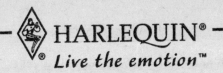

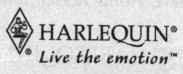

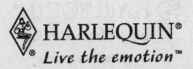

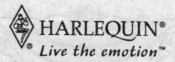

Harlequin® Historical
Historical Romantic Adventure!

*Imagine a time of chivalrous
knights and unconventional ladies,
roguish rakes and impetuous
heiresses, rugged cowboys
and spirited frontierswomen——
these rich and vivid tales will
capture your imagination!*

*Harlequin Historical . . .
they're too good to miss!*

HHDIR06